A Bonfire

A Bonfire

Pamela Hansford Johnson

M

ISBN 0 333 31138 8

First published 1981 by
MACMILLAN LONDON LIMITED
4 Little Essex Street, London WC2R 3LF
and Basingstoke
Associated companies in Delhi, Dublin,
Hong Kong, Johannesburg, Lagos, Melbourne,
New York, Singapore and Tokyo

Printed in the United States of America

Photoset in Great Britain by
ROWLAND PHOTOTYPESETTING LIMITED
Bury St Edmunds, Suffolk

To Doris Cadney,
with gratitude and love

Author's Note

The time-scheme of this book lies between 1924 and 1937. The habits, customs and amusements of the middle-class young were different from those of today.

PHJ

Part One

Chapter One

'WASTE of good water!' Miss Plimsoll cried, coming into the kitchen where Emma had been allowed to draw a glass of water but had not immediately turned the tap off. 'Waste not, want not.'

Miss Plimsoll was tall and gaunt, with a sparse bun of grey hair, pendulous cheeks criss-crossed by raspberry lines, and an almost grotesquely long upper lip. She was an old family friend, whom Emma's grandmother insisted should be visited once in a while. The visit was an imposition both to her mother and to herself, but it had to be made, and it has to be said that Emma found a good deal of comedy in Miss Plimsoll.

She lived in a small, shabby but scrupulously clean flat in a Putney side-street near the river. It was always stuffy and always depressing. 'I'm going to get tea now, so go into the front room and wait for me.'

Tea was always the same – bread-and-scrape and a few dry biscuits.

Returning with the tray, Miss Plimsoll asked Agnes Sheldrake how her husband was getting on.

'Well, of course, he has to work very hard, and things aren't easy. It was good of him to take Mother and Issie in, but it's a lot on his shoulders. He has to employ two men and a clerk now, but Issie does his typing. Anyway, that saves a salary.' Agnes was succinct. It was always as well to be so with Miss Plimsoll.

'And how is your mother?'

'She's very blind. It's sad, but we can't let her do the cooking any longer, and it was the only thing she really enjoyed.'

'We found a mouse in the rice pudding,' said Emma, who was fourteen.

'Don't be absurd, miss.'

'But we did. It was dead, of course. And cooked.'

'I'm afraid it's true,' Agnes said. Her pretty face expressed sincerity.

'So poor Grannie has nothing to do but listen to the wireless. She always stands up with the earphones on whenever they play "God Save the King". I'm the only one who can make the cat's whisker work on the crystal.'

'Hoity-toity,' said Miss Plimsoll, whose expressions tended to be years out of date.

'Emma is very clever with it,' Agnes defended her daughter. 'Reggie always has difficulty.'

'I read to her sometimes,' said Emma, 'and sing to her, too.' She had a pretty voice, which she was always eager to use. About reading aloud she was not so keen, and could rarely bring herself to do more than half an hour of it.

'Have another bit of bread-and-butter. You're too skinny and you need feeding up.' It was, in fact, bread-and-margarine, which Emma did not like. She thanked Miss Plimsoll and said she had had enough. 'A biscuit, then.' This was a dry *petit beurre*, but Emma accepted it.

'Does your husband do much business at the auction rooms?'

'Pretty fair. We get big attendances, but people don't seem to bid for much. Sometimes we get in things we should have liked ourselves, but we never seem to be able to afford them.'

'Do you remember when I was little, Mother, and I wanted a doll? You didn't buy it because, you said, "*That doll had an evil face*."'

'Well, so it had,' Agnes replied, 'but I had to say something. You were too young to understand that we couldn't afford everything.'

'I hope you're keeping up Emma's religious education.'

'She and I go to church every Sunday. Reggie says he would go, too, if they would let him smoke.' This with a fleeting smile.

'Disgusting,' said Miss Plimsoll. 'If he can't take an hour's abstinence for the sake of our Lord, what's to be made of him?'

'He thinks I do enough for us both.' Agnes, after an hour or so of this sort of thing, was provoked into some degree of impudence.

'Tush,' said Miss Plimsoll.

Emma thought how good-looking her mother was. She had small and delicate features, eyes bright but not large, and dark, almost blue-black, glossy hair. She deplored her own looks, which she thought left something to be desired. Her hair was very straight, and lighter than her mother's, and her nose was straight, too. Her eyes were larger, but of an indeterminate colour. She was just at the age to begin thinking about lovers, but as yet they were all film stars. Wallace Reid and Tom Mix. She had signed photographs of both, which were pinned to her bedroom wall. Agnes, though she watched her anxiously, did not think this was a sign of precocity. Yet Emma was precocious in her own way. She had read *Jane Eyre*, which Aunt Issie had hidden away with other forbidden books in her grandmother's Bath chair, and was half in love with Mr Rochester. She had also read *A Midsummer Night's Dream* unprompted (they had not 'done it' at school) and meant to read more of Shakespeare by herself. Her mother had once taken her to the Old Vic to see *Henry V*, and this was a treat never to be forgotten.

'How are you doing at school, Emma?' Miss Plimsoll demanded.

'Well, I'm top in English and French.'

'What about your arithmetic?'

'I'm bottom in geometry.'

'Bottom? That won't do. Perhaps your father could give you private lessons.'

'I don't think he can do geometry.'

'Suppose you say a poem to me.' This was always Miss Plimsoll's demand, and Emma was prepared for it. She stood up and recited the one about 'blind pit-ponies and little hunted hares'. It had the merit of being short.

'That all?' said Miss Plimsoll, and Emma confessed that it was. 'You'd better have something longer for me next time, and more difficult. Otherwise I shall think that you haven't much memory.'

'Emma has a good memory,' Agnes put in. 'Better than mine. It stands her in very good stead.'

'Well, I've got a present for her and I hope she deserves it.'

Miss Plimsoll brought out of a drawer a length of horrific curry-coloured cloth. 'I came across this the other day when I was clearing out. You can make her a frock of it, Agnes.'

'So kind of you. Thank Miss Plimsoll, Emma.' Agnes's voice was feeble. She knew the exigencies of her daughter's tastes.

'You could embroider it; you're good at that. A nice navy blue would look well,' suggested Miss Plimsoll.

'I suppose you're going to have a lot of banging about on Guy Fawkes Night,' Miss Plimsoll said later. 'Dreadful noise, and so dangerous. It ought to be stopped.'

'Emma will have a few of her friends in, and Reggie will let the fireworks off. He enjoys that.'

Emma, however, did not. She always put her fingers in her ears when firecrackers went off, and never relished the event until the last moment when her father energetically stamped out the bonfire in a spurting of sparks. This, at least, did not bang. She knew he enjoyed the whole thing more than she did, and that it gave him pleasure to show the garden to her school-mates, because it was bigger than most of theirs. Indeed, they often considered her well-off, with her big house, whereas in fact she was as hard up as they, and still making do with a shilling a week pocket-money. Also, some accused her of 'talking posh', though with her mother and aunt both having been on the stage they had insisted on her speaking good and clear English. She remembered having been caught at the age of four, playing with a ball and crying, 'Bahnce it! Bahnce it!' 'Say "bounce",' Aunt Issie had insisted. 'Go on, "bounce", "bounce".' These were her early-training years.

As Emma and her mother left to go, Miss Plimsoll said unexpectedly, 'She's growing up a good girl. Mind you always make her say her prayers.'

As they walked away towards the bus, Emma said, 'You're not going to make me wear that horrible material! Because I won't.'

'I shall have to make it up, though, because Miss Plimsoll will want to see it on you next time we go.'

'Do you mean I'll actually have to put it on?'

'She only meant it in kindness,' her mother said rather

feebly. 'We must be grateful to people for their good intentions. Perhaps it won't look so bad with some wool embroidery round the neck.'

They arrived home just as the auction rooms were closing for the night, and the men were putting up the shutters. The rooms were at the bottom of the Rise, equidistant between the two commons. They looked to Clapham Common to the east, and up again to St John's Church and Wandsworth Common to the west. Reggie Sheldrake came out to greet them; he was a strong-looking man with still the remains of the sunburn he had got in West Africa in his younger days. He had left there to join in the war, bringing with him a parrot and a Benin mask. Soon after enlistment, however, he was invalided out with varicose veins and had settled down to his newly acquired business. The parrot was an ill-tempered African Grey, and the mask so alarming that it had to be put on a shelf above eye-level.

Emma remembered the war with pleasure – the delectable evenings of the Zeppelin raids, when she was brought downstairs to shelter under the great mahogany sideboard. She also remembered standing with her grandmother in potato queues, and how she had enjoyed – nobody else had – eating coconut butter.

Her father kissed her. 'Well, have a rollicking time with old Miss P.?'

'She starved us,' Emma said. 'I'm famished.'

'Supper won't be long, will it, Agnes? You two go down. You'll find Grannie in the front room.'

This semi-basement room, which was backed by the kitchen and the scullery that gave on to the garden, was used for general purposes by the whole family, though it was understood that Emma's friends could take it over when they were invited. On these occasions Issie, Grannie and Reggie went to sit in the drawing-room overhead, which was rather handsome and was where Emma did her morning's freezing piano-practice.

Grannie was sitting by a highly stoked fire. She looked at Emma and her mother when they came in with eyes that were almost sightless, though she could discern their features. She

15

was a tall old woman, with her daughter's delicacy of feature and strong grey curling hair.

'And how was Ida Plimsoll?'

'Much as ever,' Agnes replied, adding mendaciously that she had sent her love. Miss Plimsoll never sent love to anyone. 'She told Emma that she was wasting good water.'

'And I only left the tap running for a moment. What's for supper?'

'Your aunt left a steak-and-kidney pudding on the stove. It should be ready in half an hour.'

'Oh, good. We had almost no tea.'

Agnes rose to draw the curtains which, to match the yellow walls, had a pattern of red and yellow autumn leaves. There was a frill of the same material round the mantelshelf.

'Well, it does her good to see you. She's lonely, poor soul. I often count my blessings.'

Which can't be many, Emma thought. Grannie could manage to find her way about the house, but all excursions had to be made in the Bath chair. Emma decided to slip out and investigate whether Aunt Issie had hidden any exciting books.

Her father came singing along the passage.

'The Law is the true embodiment
Of everything that's excellent.
It has no kind of fault or flaw,
And I, my Lords, embody the Law.'

Agnes and Issie had both been in the D'Oyly Carte company and had understudied Yum Yum and Katisha respectively, but nobody had fallen ill. Agnes had retired upon her marriage and Issie some years later, after a back injury which had left her with a slight stoop. Reggie had caught the Gilbert and Sullivan contagion from them, and Emma was often asked to play his accompaniments.

'Hullo, Gran. All well? Issie will be along in a moment; she's just finishing off some accounts. Don't sit too near the fire; I'm always afraid your skirt will catch.'

'Don't worry, Reggie, I can see how close I am. Will you light me a cigarette?' She was not allowed to use matches, but she smoked, as they all did, save Emma. This added to their reputation as a Bohemian household among Emma's friends. She fumbled for the big ashtray which Agnes had set beside her. 'After supper, Emma, I'd like you to put my record on the gramophone.' This was the boy soprano, Ernest Lough, singing 'Oh, for the Wings of a Dove'. 'And then you might fix my wireless. It's Mabel Constanduros tonight.' Grannie always went to her bedroom to listen, which she shared with Issie on the ground floor back. 'It's been a long day,' she added rather fretfully.

'Never mind, Gran, we're all here now. And here's Issie.'

Issie had paused while coming along the passage. Emma hoped she had deposited a new book.

Isabel had her grandmother's curly hair, but not her sister's delicate features.

'We sold that walnut chiffonier today,' she said to Agnes. 'It went for six pounds, but the bidding was slow. There doesn't seem to be much money about.'

Emma took advantage of the general talk to slip out into the hall and investigate the Bath chair. Yes, there was a new book, *Mademoiselle de Maupin*, translated from the French. She did not think it looked very interesting.

When she returned to the front room she collided with Issie, who was coming out of the door. Emma had only just returned in time. 'I'm just coming to see to the pudding,' her aunt said. 'You can come and lay the table. We'll eat in the kitchen tonight.' They always had breakfast and midday dinner at the big kitchen-table. Supper was usually served in the front room.

'Church tomorrow,' she added, as Emma went to and fro. 'Mind you attend to Mr Mossop; he preaches a good sermon.'

'Yes, but he dribbles and his little beard gets wet.'

'You oughtn't to criticise a good man like that. You're getting far too critical lately.' Aunt Issie, too, could be captious.

The others came in for the meal. Reggie served it, and Agnes cut up her mother's food for her.

'Hungry, everyone?'

'I am, Daddy, and I expect Mother is, too.'

17

'But don't give me too much,' said Agnes. 'I don't want to get fat.'

He served them all with pudding, mashed potatoes and the Brussels sprouts which Emma did not like but was made to eat. They were good for her, she was told.

'I'll put the gas-fire on in the drawing-room. I want Emma to accompany me in "The Nightmare Song". I think I can manage it all now, and Gran says the Moffats are coming for a musical evening on Friday. You can stay up that night, Stick-in-the-Mud,' he said to his daughter, 'and you can sing, too.'

'I don't care for George Moffat,' Grannie said. 'He always brings the same old song. I must have heard it a dozen times.'

But Emma was delighted. She always found these evenings great fun, and was glad to show off herself. After supper she attended to Grannie's wireless and went upstairs to the first floor for a protracted bath. She and her parents had their bedrooms there. The top two floors of the house were kept furnished for lodgers, but at present were empty. Tomorrow she would walk on the common with her friend Floss White, and bring her home to tea.

Chapter Two

SCHOOL. Monday. First period, English, with Miss Sumnour. Subject, *Macbeth*.

Miss Sumnour, perambulating the daïs, blonde cropped hair, sharp features, was longing to begin. This was her favourite form (V*a*), her favourite play, her favourite pupil, Emma Sheldrake.

'This is a play in two colours, black and red. The black of night, the red of blood. It is, as Shakespeare might have said, "imbrued with blood". When Macbeth goes "the primrose way to the everlasting bonfire", he is treading in blood all the way.'

At this point Floss White, in the back row, keeled over in a faint.

Miss Sumnour had not remembered, or perhaps had never known, Floss's peculiarity, which was to be unable to bear the sight of, or even the mention of, blood. This gave her two days off school at the beginning of each menstrual period.

'Girls! Lay Florence flat on the floor and lift her feet higher than her head. You can put my cushion under her. Alice, run upstairs and fetch Nurse. Now, what set her off like that?'

'She can't bear anyone to mention blood, Miss Sumnour,' said Emma.

'Oh dear, and how is she going to get through *Macbeth*? I suppose she could go to V*b*; they're doing *The Tempest* this term, which ought to be harmless. It's the same period as mine, too.' She went to help the girls lift Floss's feet even higher. 'There will be complications about the set book, but that can't be helped. I believe she's coming round.'

Nurse came in and took charge. In a few moments Floss was on her feet, weeping. 'Oh, I don't know what came over me. I'm so sorry, Miss Sumnour.'

'You couldn't help it. Take her to lie down for the rest of the morning, Nurse.'

When they had gone she turned back to her class with relief. 'Now, let's get on. We've wasted enough time already. Have any of you read *Macbeth* before? You, Emma? Well, it will be the more interesting for you to hear it analysed, don't you think?' She told the class that it was the shortest of Shakespeare's plays and would seem the most full of 'quotations'. She was a good teacher, and the class soon recovered itself from the dramatic incident of Floss's faint. 'It opens in darkness and torrential rain. The three witches are sitting round the cauldron. We'll read it in parts. You, Alice, first witch, Anna the second, Mildred the third. And try to put some expression in it.'

They continued happily enough until it was time to go to Miss Peterson for mathematics. 'And don't look so lugubrious, Emma,' Miss Sumnour said. 'You know you can do them if you concentrate.'

'I hate geometry. It's all right when they use the letters *PQR*, because I can learn a theorem off by heart. But then they change them to *ABC* and I'm all thrown out.'

'Well, better luck next time. I shall see you all tomorrow.'

At the morning's break for milk and biscuits, Emma was joined by Floss, who had not wanted to lie down for longer; she felt all right now. Floss White was a tall, etiolated, pasty girl with fine hair and eyes. She was totally without humour, and Agnes and Reggie could not imagine what their daughter saw in her. Nor could Emma, really. It was as though Floss was a henchman, rather than a friend. Perhaps the real secret was that in one respect only Floss was more mature than Emma, and longed for a real boyfriend. So at Floss's instigation they walked the common together on Sunday afternoons hoping to be picked up by two boys from the grammar school. This had not happened yet.

'All covered with blood!' a malicious girl said in a thrilling whisper as she went by, and Floss all but fainted again.

'Christabel, you beast!' Emma cried. 'Don't you dare do that again!'

'Oh, she only does it to be different,' Christabel jeered, and she ran off.

'Sit down, Floss, and finish your milk.' They sat on the edge of the gymnasium daïs. 'You must be fit for our fireworks party. Daddy has got a whole lot, and Mother's making us a guy.'

'I'll bring some, too. All the girls will. I heard them saying so.'

The gymnasium was large and well equipped, with wall-bars, boom and ropes. Emma was poor at gym, except that she could climb ropes better than anyone else. 'That's because you're descended from a monkey,' Christabel had said. Emma always landed in the middle of the vaulting-horse, which she detested. The bell signalled the end of break, and Emma and Floss went upstairs to the science room for biology.

'Matric next year,' said Emma. 'Thank heavens it'll be another set book.'

'It'll be awful if they set *Macbeth*,' Floss said apprehensively. 'I'd be sure to fail.'

'No, you'll be quite safe. Miss Sumnour says they'll be setting *A Midsummer Night's Dream*, and there's nothing to make you faint in that.' They hastily finished their milk and biscuits and climbed to the top of the building.

It was Guy Fawkes Night on the following Friday, and Emma had invited seven of her friends.

'I don't know how I'm going to behave myself among such a bevy of female beauty,' said her father. '"Put me among the girls,"' he sang. 'Your mother's taken my old tweed trousers for your guy, and they were the most comfortable I had.'

They were to have chestnuts and potatoes baked in the ashes of the bonfire, though Grannie said both would be as hard as iron. Aunt Issie offered partially to cook the potatoes in the oven. She had baked two dozen jam tarts.

'And mind you all wrap up warm,' said Agnes. 'I do hope it's not going to rain.'

But it did not, since an early drizzle gave way to clearer skies.

The guy, made by her out of two worn-out pillows, a pair of socks stuffed with straw, and a pink and white mask topped by an old tam-o'-shanter of Emma's, was a fine sight.

'Aren't you clever, Mamma! The girls will love it!'

The bonfire was lit at seven o'clock, by which time the guests had arrived. It caught fire at once, throwing a fantasy of shadows over the garden. Agnes put the half-baked potatoes and chestnuts beneath it. Floss had bought a packet of sparklers and she shared them out, so that they could all wave them as they danced about the fire. Grannie came muffled up against the cold, feeling her way down the stone steps. She could see the glow, the whirling sparklers and the outlines of the dancing girls.

'"The everlasting bonfire,"' Emma remembered, and felt a chill. Agnes, to make up for Reggie's indifference, had done her best to make Emma religious, whatever her opinion of Mr Mossop and his beard. She had succeeded, and Emma was to be confirmed that year. Agnes knew that she had her doubts. When she recited the Creed she always left something out, and had honestly said that she could not believe in several of the Thirty-Nine Articles. But she believed in everything else – in the New Testament, that was, because Mr Mossop was far from being a fundamentalist – and said her prayers with fervour. She believed in Heaven and Hell, and would have liked to be permitted to believe in Purgatory, which seemed to her a humane and reasonable half-way house, but Mr Mossop's roads did not lead to Rome. When she had spoken to her mother about Hell, Agnes had said awkwardly that she believed our punishment for our sins was in our own lives. 'But Mr Mossop doesn't seem to believe that,' said Emma.

'You don't have to take seriously all old Mossop says,' Reggie put in easily.

'Reggie!' said his wife. 'Don't you teach Emma to go against Mr Mossop.'

'Well, my dear, I thought that was what you were doing. Have a cigarette; it'll calm you down.'

Agnes thought it would, and she accepted.

It was time to set off the fireworks. 'Would you like to go in, Gran?' said Reggie.

'No, I wouldn't. I may even be able to see some of them, and I shall hear the bangs.'

He set off the first of them, a magnificent Golden Rain,

which exploded at the top of the sky then showered down in floods of gold to a chorus of 'oohs' and 'ahs'.

'I could just see that,' said Grannie, 'or I thought I could.'

Next, a spray of emerald stars, and then a series of fire-crackers, spraying their lights from the ground. Emma, in the darkness of the garden, put her fingers in her ears. She longed for this part of the ceremony to be over. But her father was enjoying himself. He had collected the offerings of the guests and had ranged them in order. From other gardens came bangs and soaring lights, but none seemed as fine as theirs. When it was all over, Aunt Issie brought out her jam tarts and took the potatoes and chestnuts from the bonfire.

'That was marvellous,' said Agnes, and the girls echoed her.

By this time the guy had properly caught fire, and the smell of burning feathers and wool pervaded the garden. The pink and white mask crumpled and blackened, and Emma's tam-o'-shanter curled and disintegrated. Agnes whispered to Emma, 'Pity Floss can't faint here. They say it pulls you round if they burn feathers under your nose.'

Reggie came at last in his gardening-boots to stamp the flames out. The sparks flew, to Emma's delight, and the remainder of the guy toppled over into the ashes.

'Now, girls,' said Agnes, 'you all come indoors and warm yourselves up.'

'We got warm by the bonfire, Mrs Sheldrake,' said Floss.

'But I think it's going to rain again. I can feel it spitting.'

So they all made their way into the basement front room, and Reggie told them to put their coats down on the table. It was pleasant in the warm light. Despite their claims of having been warm enough in the garden, the girls were glad enough to hold their hands out to the fire. Aunt Issie brought in sausage rolls and a jug of hot chocolate.

'This is a regular feast,' said Mildred. 'Thank you, Miss Hewitt.'

'It's rather topsy-turvy, though,' Issie answered. 'Sausage rolls after jam tarts.'

'It's a pity old Mossop wasn't here,' said Reggie jovially, as he came in out of the dark, his cheeks glowing. 'He'd love to burn Papists.'

23

Emma plucked at his sleeve to stop him. Mildred was a Roman Catholic, though this did not seem to interfere with her pleasure at Guy Fawkes Nights.

'I am sure Mr Mossop would not be so cruel,' said Grannie, in a tone of reproof.

'Have a cigarette, Gran?'

'Not just now, thank you, Reggie.' She did not care to smoke before Emma's friends, though Agnes had and Issie did not mind. The girls watched them, somewhat awestruck, as they lit up.

'Now, how are you all going to get home?' Agnes asked. 'I know several of you live the same way. But Mildred goes in the other direction, and I don't like to see her go by herself after dark.'

Reggie said that he could set her on her way.

'Oh, there's no need for that, Mr Sheldrake. My mother never worries if I'm out a bit late.'

'So we'll give her no chance to worry at all, shall we?'

At last, with profuse thanks, they were all gone. Grannie and Aunt Issie had gone up to bed, Reggie was still out seeing Mildred home, and Emma prepared herself for a talk with her mother before the fire.

The question had been put into her mind on the previous Sunday, when Mr Mossop had preached on the Ten Commandments.

'Mamma, I want to ask you something.'

She paused. Agnes was apprehensive, as she knew what these questions could be like. 'Go ahead, darling.'

'Exactly what *is* adultery?'

Agnes always liked to give the appearance of frankness. Nevertheless, she was taken aback.

'What made you think about that?'

'It was while we were in the garden. What is it, please? I don't like not to know.'

'It means sleeping with a man to whom you aren't married.'

'Yes, but just sleeping? Lying down and going to sleep?'

Agnes marvelled at such innocence. She had, in a rather cowardly way, hoped that Emma had already known the truth from one of her schoolfriends.

She began diffidently, 'You know that men are made differently from women?'

Emma did. She had seen a baby cousin in his bath. She persisted with her question. Agnes answered it, with great difficulty and with little finesse.

'And is it nice?' Emma said at last. She was trying to repress a repugnance towards her parents.

'If married people love each other, it is. Some people don't care for it much.'

'And that's the way you get babies?'

'Yes.'

'I think', said Emma, 'that I would rather be a nun.'

Agnes was not dismayed by this response, considering Emma temperamentally unfitted for the cloister.

'Let's talk of something else, darling, and don't let it prey on your mind. Your father will be back soon.'

When he came in, it had been raining.

'Hullo, old girl,' he said to Agnes. And 'Hullo, Tuppence,' to Emma. 'Lucky we started early or we should have been drowned out. I saw Silly Millie right to her front door. Well, I think it went off all right, don't you?'

'Thank you,' said Emma stiffly.

He stared at her. 'Has your old father done something wrong?'

'No. It was fine. They all enjoyed themselves.' She had difficulty in forcing the words out.

'You sound funny. What's the matter?'

'Nothing, I'm just tired.'

'Then perhaps you'd better go on up. Perhaps we all had.' He sounded disappointed. It had always been one of the pleasures of a party to talk it over. 'I'll rake out the fire.'

He knelt to do so. 'No chance for Floss to faint tonight,' he said.

Emma forced a laugh.

'Gran seems to have enjoyed herself. She says she could see the big rockets. Do you think they had enough to eat?' he asked Agnes.

'Plenty. Emma and I finished off the sausage rolls.'

'I think I will go up, Daddy. I shouldn't be surprised if I had a cold coming on.'

'So that's what's wrong with you. Now we know. I don't suppose being in the garden on a November night did it much good. Give me a kiss.'

Emma did so and retired to her small bedroom on the first floor. Her parents had the large one at the back.

In the darkness she pondered Agnes's revelations. To think that her own mother and father – but, she recollected sensibly, if they hadn't she would not have been born. How repulsive nature was! People must be doing this thing all over the world. Agnes had omitted to tell her that the penis grew, and Emma, thinking of her baby cousin, marvelled that so small a thing could have such effects. But, then, as a man grew so must it grow. Emma hoped her parents had given up such practices since her own birth. For surely there could be no further use for them?

She was an innocent girl and had an inward chill that had made her more knowledgeable schoolfriends hesitant to confide in her. Now, she felt, she knew as much as they did.

On Sunday she and her mother would wheel Grannie up to church. Aunt Issie would stay behind to cook the Sunday joint, with Yorkshire pudding. And in the afternoon a walk with Floss White, and perhaps they would at last pick up some boys. She did not think what her parents would have said had they known the object of these expeditions.

Chapter Three

EMMA tossed and turned and could not get to sleep. She lay on her back, watching the lights from the passing buses swerve across the ceiling. She could not forget her mother's revelations, which were now mingled with the memory of the fireworks and the shrivelling guy. An hour passed, and two, and she heard her father come out of his bedroom and fumble his way downstairs. There was electric light only in the basement and on the ground floor: gas lit all the rest. 'We can't afford the lot,' Reggie had said, and Gran had lamented, 'A pound a point! A pound a point!'

It had been a long time since her father had gone down, and she suddenly began to worry. She put on her dressing-gown and slippers and crept after him, hoping all the time to hear his smoker's cough; if she did, she could beat a retreat. The light was burning in the ground-floor passage, and she saw at once that he had fallen outside the lavatory door. He was lying on his face, and she could not turn him over. He did not seem to be breathing, and she was terrified. She rushed upstairs and into her parents' bedroom, where her mother was fast asleep. 'Wake up, please wake up! Daddy's fallen down outside the lavatory, and I can't get him to move! You must come at once.'

Agnes knelt by the body of her husband and tried to feel his pulse. She began to cry. 'Reggie, Reggie, wake up!'

Emma said, 'I'd better call Aunt Issie.'

'Ring Dr Carson first and tell him to come at once.'

'Is Daddy dead?'

'I don't know.' But Agnes had caught a glimpse of his face, and she knew.

Emma went to the bottom of the basement stairs where the telephone was inconveniently installed, and roused the doctor from his sleep. Then she went to wake her aunt, taking care not to wake her grandmother, who was getting very deaf.

When Issie saw the body she fell on her knees beside it. She had always loved Reggie and it had been a great disappointment to her when he had chosen Agnes.

Emma could not cry; she was being too active. She could not leave them till the doctor came.

He was a tall, dark, radish-like man who had come out in his pyjamas and top-coat. He examined Reggie with care and turned him on to his back. 'I think he's had a heart-attack,' he said. 'Emma had better call an ambulance.' He gave Agnes and Issie what comfort he could. The grandfather clock struck two.

When she knew the ambulance was on its way she returned to the ground floor. Nobody thought to send her to bed but Dr Carson.

'Look, Emma, there's no sense in your staying here. Just try to get back to sleep.'

She went reluctantly, having found death exciting. She would weep later.

Next morning, exhausted, she slept late. Her mother, in a bright-coloured jacket, brought her a cup of tea.

'Perhaps Floss will have you for the day. She's on the phone, so I'll call her mother and see.'

'But I don't want to be sent away!'

'There's nothing more you can do here.'

'Mother, why are you wearing that coat?'

'It was all I could find. Besides, I didn't want to upset you still more. It's a dreadful blow, darling, but I'm going to be both father and mother to you now.'

'Did he suffer much pain?'

'I don't think so. It was all very sudden. I'll write a note to school saying that you'll be away next week. Come down as soon as you can and have some breakfast and then you can dress and get off.'

The day was a Saturday, so Floss's mother was able to take Emma. Reluctantly she left Agnes and Aunt Issie behind to cope with all there was to be done. Dr Carson signed the death certificate, and the body was brought home to lie upstairs. By the time she arrived home from a gloomy day with Floss, the others had recovered much of their equilibrium and only Grannie still wept, sitting alone in the drawing-room. Emma offered to read to her.

'I couldn't take it in, dear. Just let me be quiet here. I was so fond of your father; he was such a merry man.'

For the first time Emma fell to crying. She was just recovering from the initial shock.

'Is everything being done? I feel so old and useless. It's dreadful to be blind.'

'I know it is, Grannie, I know it is.'

She went downstairs to where Agnes and Issie were desultorily eating some supper. 'There's a pie in the oven for you,' Agnes said. 'You must have something to eat. And tell us what flowers you'll want to send to the funeral. Now, do stop crying. There's still plenty to be done.'

'We shall have to sell the business,' Issie said. 'Mr Beddoes and I can look after it for a day or two.'

'But we can keep on the house?' asked Emma.

'If we possibly can. But it has always gone with the auction rooms before.'

Emma wondered at the practical problems death brought, and thought it as well for everyone to have something to think about. She managed to eat about half her pie and to tell her mother she would like to send violets. Her father was still very much alive to her; at any moment she would hear his dry, short cough upon the stairs.

'I wonder if last night's exertions brought it on?' Issie said. She was crying again, but in a stifled way. 'He was dancing around just like a boy at that bonfire, when he was stamping it out.'

'Then it's good to think that his last evening was a happy one,' said Agnes, with just a touch of annoyance. 'Emma's friends saw him at his best.'

The day of the funeral was bright, and mild for the time of year. Agnes and Issie were in heavy mourning, but Emma just had a black band round the arm of her school coat. There were only themselves and a few distant relations, Reggie having had no parents living. There were many wreaths on the coffin, from his widow and sister-in-law, a bunch of violets from Emma and more wreaths from his clerk, his masonic friends and some local tradesmen. Grannie was left behind with a neighbour for company. The service was at St Mark's Church, the interment in the nearby cemetery. Emma listened with appreciation to the ceremony, which was conducted by Mr Mossop, and afterwards went with the others to the committal to earth. It seemed to her awful that a lively man like her father should be dumped into the ground. She had been given back her violets to drop on top of the coffin. 'Ashes to ashes. . . .' She seemed almost to hear her father laugh at this brusque arrangement for his disposal. If only he had been allowed to smoke in church!

They all came home to the customary cold collation, over which Grannie managed to preside. Pork pies, ham, chicken, fruit salad, trifle. It all seemed to Emma rather heathenish, especially as her mother and Aunt Issie were visibly shaken after the morning. She herself had worked up an appetite, which she had managed partially to conceal. She was friendly with all the vague relations and won their approval.

At last they all left, and Agnes and Issie devoted themselves to the washing-up. They had a daily girl, but she had been given the day off.

Next week, Emma went back to school. She was received with unwonted respect, and was reminded of David Copperfield, to whom the death of a much-loved mother seemed to have given an altogether not unenjoyable status. There was some talk of their electing her form-captain next term. But that, she felt, was some way off, and she doubted the stalwartness of their resolution.

By the mistresses she found herself let off unpleasant things, such as the boom and the horse and netball. It would not last, but it was nice while it did. Floss also had a special position, having been the first to succour the bereaved. Emma, who usually took a penny bus at the bottom of the hill to home, walked across the common with her and was just in time to see the sun sink behind St Mark's and the masonic school into the colours of a Neapolitan ice: chocolate, pistachio and rose. They were also in time to see some of the grammar-school boys, a few of whom they knew, pedalling up the steep hill on their bicycles.

'Do you feel awfully bad?' said Floss, who could never leave well alone.

'I shall get used to it in time,' Emma replied, in an appropriately mournful tone.

'It was fine when your father met us from school and took us home by way of Webbs Road, and always bought us sweets. We all thought he was wonderful.'

'And so he was,' said Emma.

They managed to sell the auction rooms for a fair price and let the first, second and third floors of the house. It was arranged that Agnes and Emma should make their bedroom, sharing a double bed, in the former sitting-room, which would still be large enough to serve for social purposes.

This sharing of a bed was not to Emma's liking. 'Oh, do have your hair cut, Mamma! Your plait keeps getting into my mouth.'

It was a shock to find that Reggie had left only five hundred pounds and that he still owed money to bookmakers. He had always been an unlucky gambler.

However, with the sale of the auction rooms and the rentals, they found themselves fairly comfortably off. Agnes took in typing, and Issie was kept on in her job, salaried this time. Emma was wanting smarter dresses than those her mother could now make for her, so was allowed to go to Miss Serin, the 'little dressmaker' up the Rise. Emma drew designs for her dresses, which Miss Serin interpreted with some degree of clairvoyance.

'Emma designs her own clothes,' Agnes said proudly to friends.

She indulged her daughter a good deal now, letting her have friends in one evening a week – three girls and two properly accredited boys who were members of St Mark's congregation – and they rolled up the carpet and danced, trying to learn the Charleston. One of the boys was a long-nosed blond called Leslie McNab, who was thought rather an ass by his schoolmates but was, at sixteen, an excellent dancer. He even taught Agnes to dance, she being always in the role of chaperon. 'No,

Mrs Sheldrake, *smooth, smooth*, two quick, one slow.' She was an apt pupil. She gave them tea and their favourite bread pudding – a confection of bread soaked in milk with spices, brown sugar and sultanas. It was good cold.

At ten o'clock Issie would come in and meaningfully put the clock on the sideboard. This annoyed Agnes, but much amused the boys and girls.

Emma was fifteen now, not pretty, but handsome in a rather severe way, and she had learned to do her hair more becomingly. Altogether it was a happy time for her.

Chapter Four

IN THE NEXT YEAR she began studying for matriculation, taking private lessons in the hope of being able to understand algebra and geometry. This cost Agnes a good deal, but it seemed to her worth it. It did not seem so to Emma, who drove to despair the elderly professor who was teaching her. He finally told Agnes that he had no hope of success. 'Your daughter seems to me mentally defective in the mathematical part of her brain, though otherwise her intellect is excellent.'

So Emma could not matriculate, but had to be content with a General Schools Certificate with distinction in English, French, Latin and Art. This gave her a move into the sixth form, though to her great disappointment she was not made a prefect and could not wear the coveted silver medal. But she enjoyed the liberty to work in free periods and, besides, she was in love.

He was Leslie McNab, and she walked the common no longer. Her friendship with Floss White had wilted, partly on this account, and partly because Floss, who had become very religious, had attached herself to the pietistic Violet Grant, whom Emma could not endure.

'Emma Sheldrake, whenever I hear you say "blast" I can see a black cloud forming round your mouth.'

'Oh, shut up, Violet, you're too pi.'

Agnes deplored her passion for Leslie, thinking her far too young to dream of such things. When she allowed him to take Emma to a dance at the town hall, it was on condition that she accompanied them, which much spoiled Emma's pleasure.

Emma was aware of her mother's possessiveness, but did not mind much if her friends didn't. Since her father's death this had grown perceptibly, Agnes wanting to go with her everywhere. She sometimes dreamed of being quite alone, but a dream this remained. Agnes was omnipresent. Leslie, despite his nose, was the best-looking boy there and of course the best dancer. He had taught Emma, who was not a natural dancer, to some effect, and made her do the spectacular Argentine tango and the Yale Blues.

'Dear little one,' he would murmur as he swept her round the floor, 'you are doing me proud.'

At the beginning of September she fell ill. Leslie was distraught. Meeting her friend Ann Clifford on the Rise he said passionately, 'My girl's dying.'

'Oh, is she? What of?'

'Mumps,' said Leslie and was distressed when Ann went off into a fit of laughter.

Agnes was distressed that Emma had to miss church. When she was up again, she took her into the drawing-room and suggested that she and Grannie and her daughter had a little private service on their own. She read a prayer, and made them join in her favourite hymn, 'The King of Love My Shepherd Is'. She even gave them a short sermon. All this embarrassed Emma dreadfully, and she was determined not to participate again if her mother attempted a repeat performance. But Agnes, sensing this had not been altogether a success, did not.

It was after her recovery from mumps that Emma tired of Leslie. His 'dear little girl' and 'sweet small thing' had ceased to have their charm for her. And so she made closer friends with Ann, whose boys were older and did not make silly speeches.

'It's no good, Leslie, I just don't feel the same any more.'

'Don't say that, little girl,' he responded, his big blue eyes full of tears. 'I was training you to be my dancing partner. Soon we could give exhibitions.'

'You can train other girls, better than I am.'

'You're good enough for me.'

'I'm sorry, Leslie, but I want to be alone for a while.'

'There's someone else!'

'No, there isn't. I mean what I say.'

So poor Leslie was banished.

Agnes and Emma were asked down for a week-end at the riverside bungalow of Eric Flowers, an old family friend. 'It would be fun,' Emma said. 'Do let's go.'

The bungalow was a large one, near Walton. When they arrived there, they found a crowd of young men and women putting up lanterns and fairy lights. Eric, a dapper young–old man in white flannels, explained. 'We're having a dance on the veranda tonight. You must both be at your best. Why, Emma, how you've grown! I should never have known you. Come and see your room. It's been thoroughly dried out.'

Emma was shy of the men and women at first, feeling them very sophisticated. She was glad that she was wearing Miss Serin's latest concoction, a summer dress of blue and green, pleated to just below the knee. It was as smart as anyone's. 'Come on,' said a young man, sweeping her to her feet, 'let's practise for this evening. Can you Charleston?'

Emma said she had tried, feeling flattered that he should have asked her. He wound up the gramophone and came to her again.

The river ran sunnily with its fleet of swans. Eric's two dinghies were moored at the landing-stage.

'Put your hands on my shoulders,' said the young man. 'You'll see better how it goes.' So Emma did so, and jerked her knees according to his example. 'You're doing fine,' he said.

He left with his friends for lunch. 'See you tonight,' he called, 'and save a dance for me.'

'You've made a conquest,' Eric exclaimed. 'He doesn't usually strike up a friendship so easily. How old are you?'

'Nearly sixteen.'

He said, to her pleasure, 'You look more. Your mother's as young as she ever was.'

She looked forward to the evening. The effect was magical when the lanterns were lit, reflected in the river, and when the men and girls came back. She looked eagerly for Stephen Hood, as Eric had told her he was called, and when she saw him he smiled and waved to her. She was able now to re-member what he looked like – blunt but delicate features, reddish hair. There was only room for four couples to dance on the veranda at one time, but some of the dancers continued in the fairly large front room. Eric took charge of the gramo-phone and only danced once himself, with Agnes.

Stephen said to Emma, 'Let's wait a little. I want to know all about you. How old you are.' She answered with a little exaggeration. 'And I'm twenty-one. An old man.' She laughed at this and asked him about himself. He had been to a minor public school and was now working in a bank. He liked dancing, but only with the right partner. 'That's you,' he said, 'and no one else is going to have a chance. Shall we dare to Charleston?'

She did dare, and found herself better at it than he was. When they sat down again Agnes, ever watchful, joined them. Emma introduced her mother.

'You're a good dancer yourself, Mrs Sheldrake,' he said admiringly.

'I was in Gilbert and Sullivan years ago,' she replied, 'and we had to dance then.'

Eric brought out a tray of cocktails. Agnes took one, but said doubtfully to Emma, 'I don't think you ought.'

'Oh, Mother, please!'

'Yes, do let her,' said Stephen. 'One won't hurt her.'

So Emma had her first cocktail and, though she did not like it much, was flattered to be allowed to have it.

A young man came up and asked Agnes to dance. 'I'm afraid I've danced enough already.'

'But not with me. Please don't say no.'

Nobody but Stephen asked Emma; she was partly discountenanced and partly happy. 'Your mother's quite a success,' he said.

'More than I am,' she said naïvely.

'If the men don't come to you, it's because I freeze them off with my glare. Do you know you're the best-looking girl in the whole place?'

'I'm going to have a perm soon. I'm looking forward to that.'

'You may spoil yourself. I like you as you are. Shall we meet again in London? Here, it's a lovely night. Let's go and walk in the garden.'

So they slipped away down the wooden steps and went into the shadow of the trees.

'I'm going to kiss you,' he said, and did.

'No, you mustn't do that. We hardly know each other.'

'But we're going to know each other very well, aren't we?'

'I don't know.' She was terrified lest Agnes should pursue them. 'People will be looking for us. We must get back.'

But the heat and the magic of the moment had lured other couples beside themselves into the darkness of the garden. With difficulty she persuaded him to join the dancers again. When they did so they found Agnes sitting by herself. Seeing them, she looked relieved.

'I don't think your mother trusts me,' said Stephen, 'though I'm the most trustworthy man on earth.'

'Where have you two been?' Agnes asked.

'Just for a little walk,' he answered. 'It got so stuffy in here.'

'Mamma, may I have another cocktail?' Eric had come out again with another tray. He winked at Emma.

'No, you may not,' Agnes said firmly. 'No, Mr Hood,' she said to Stephen, 'I won't have you encouraging her. I don't like to see her drink.'

And for the rest of that evening she seldom left them alone except to dance, and they managed little but to exchange addresses.

Emma was still excited by the music, the lanterns, the fairy lamps, and by Stephen's kiss, though it had been a gentle one. She wished the evening would go on for ever. She wished her mother would go away. She wondered whether she was in love again.

By one o'clock in the morning, the men and girls had all gone back to their own bungalows or had ferried themselves home across the river.

'That was a lovely party,' she said to Eric, who had brought them out cups of tea.

'We must go to bed,' Agnes said. 'Emma has never stayed up so late.'

'Well, let her make it ten minutes later, as an additional treat. Have you danced a lot?'

'Almost off my feet. Those boys were kind to an old woman.'

'Old, my foot,' he said. 'You might be Emma's sister.'

'Don't flatter, Eric. I'm at least too old for that.'

But Emma saw that her mother was pleased. She wondered

whether she could ever marry again, decided that she would not mind if she did. At least it would take her mind off her daughter.

'There's going to be a big dance at the boathouse tomorrow. This little affair was only a warm-up. We shall all go.'

Emma prayed that Stephen would be there. He had not mentioned another dance to her.

There were lanterns here, too, and balloons hanging from the ceiling. There was a three-piece band, and the floor glistened with chalk. Eric introduced her to a stoutish young man whom she knew to be quite a well-known actor. He danced clumsily, remarking, 'This is a boopsy tune, eh?' She was proud to be seen with him, but he was hard on her feet. When she returned to her seat she was glad of the rest, and hoped that, for the moment, Eric would introduce no one else.

Then she saw Stephen. He was dancing with a tall girl in a long dress, and Emma's heart sank. How could she hope to attract him now? She was wearing a yellow frock, her newest, but it could not match this girl's. She and Stephen circulated the floor three or four times, and then he took her back to her seat and came straight to Emma and her mother. 'I didn't see you before. Are you having a good time? Perhaps you'll dance with me first, Mrs Sheldrake.' Agnes, surprised and flustered, rose at once. Emma saw them talking together, and envied her mother's grace. Taught by poor Leslie, too, she thought. She waited for someone to claim her, but no one did. Eric was dancing with a chorus girl who had taken his fancy.

When Stephen and Agnes came back he sat down beside them. 'I was asking your mother whether I could call on you both when we're back in Town.'

Agnes was obviously taken aback by this old-fashioned courtesy. She said ineptly, 'Emma is still at school, you know.'

'But it's my last term, Mamma.'

'My sister's only just left. I must introduce her to you.' He indicated the girl with whom Emma had just seen him, and her heart rose. 'I can't tear Sylvia away from her partners now, but

I will in the interval. This is a Yale Blues, Emma. Shall we dance it?'

She was moving delightfully with him again, and thought he smelled sweet, like hay. The night was humid. 'When this one's over, shall we go out and walk on the bank?'

'But my mother—'

'She won't be lonely. Do come.'

But she would not. She was not going to be too easy: her mother had taught her this. 'Never let a boy be too sure of you,' she had said. Emma reflected that Leslie had been far too sure of her.

In the interval he brought his sister over. 'Mrs Sheldrake, this is Sylvia. Emma.'

Sylvia had a broad, good-humoured face, and her fair hair was cut short. She shook hands with a boyish grip, and said to her brother, 'Steve, don't just stand there. Go and get us some ices. He always has to be prodded,' she confided to Emma. 'Perhaps you'd rather have lemonade, though? There's no licence here, but some of them go over the river to the Dragon.'

'Lemonade, please,' said Emma, and Stephen went off with their orders. Sylvia confided, 'He's my big brother. Only by two years, though. So I can bully him. Have you any brothers or sisters?'

'Alas, she's an only one,' Agnes answered for Emma.

'That must have been fun, though, to have all the attention. There are three of us, and the youngest is only eleven. He's called Noel, and he's the bright one. He's brilliant at school, which I can't say for Steve and me.' She chattered on gaily until he returned, and Emma warmed to her.

'Emma and I are going to Charleston, Syl,' he said. 'I bet she's better at it than you are.'

'Anyone would be. I'll watch out for you.'

Emma wondered how many girls Stephen had had, and wondered whether Sylvia had been so welcoming to all of them. She would have liked her for a friend.

When they came back to their seats, Stephen said to Agnes, 'Emma and I are going for a walk on the river bank. Would you like to come, too?'

Agnes was flustered. 'No, I don't think I will, thank you. It's getting late.'

'Oh, not yet awhile! I'll take good care of Emma, Mrs Sheldrake.'

Emma said, when she and Stephen were alone in the semi-darkness, the swans and the music drifting past them, 'You ought to have asked me.'

'And got another refusal? No, I want to hear all about you.'

Coaxed, she told him about her friends, about the weekly bread-pudding party, about poor Leslie. She also told him about her other friends, Ann, Silly Millie, Dicky Striver and Donald Hume, who was an intellectual.

'When I come,' said Stephen, 'I'm going to get rid of Leslie, and Dicky and Donald.'

'But Leslie's gone.'

'Well, that's one the less.' Taking an empty cigarette-box from his pocket, he tore off a strip of the silver paper and made it into a ring. He put it on the third finger of her left hand. 'That's a promise.'

She gave it back to him. 'I can't be seen with this.'

'You shall be seen with something like it another time.'

He kissed her again. 'Now we'd better be getting back, or your mother will be worrying, and I wouldn't want her to do that.'

When they got back to the boathouse, they found Agnes dancing in a distracted way with Eric, her eyes ever on the door. 'I told you,' said Stephen.

The band was playing 'Good-night, Sweetheart,' and it was time to go.

'So I may come and see you, Mrs Sheldrake?' he asked.

'Perhaps you would bring your sister.'

'Well, she works at Walton and it's a long way for her to come. But I'm sure she'd love to, if she can.'

When Emma was in bed that night, her mother came to sit by her.

'Listen, darling. I don't want you to get involved with that young man. He's too old for you and, besides, he's a bit too sure of himself.'

Emma thought of her paper ring. 'But didn't you like him?'

40

'He was very polite, and I expect he's very nice. But you are so young.'

'I shan't always be young,' Emma said, simulating a yawn.

Chapter Five

IT WAS nearly two weeks before she heard from Stephen again, and she was in despair. Then she had a letter, obviously designed to be shown to her mother.

Dear Emma,
. . . May I come to one of your weekly parties? I promise to like all your friends. Do let me, and ask your mother if I can come, too.

Ever yours,
Stephen

'Not many boys would be so considerate,' Agnes admitted. 'Tell him he can come, then, and don't let him expect too much. He may not like the bed being in the sitting-room, or Issie coming in with the clock. I do wish she wouldn't.'

When he arrived he came up the front steps, and so was taken to the drawing-room to be introduced to Grannie and Issie. He was deferential. When Grannie asked him, as was now her custom, if she might feel his features in order to know what he looked like, he knelt before her like a knight at vigil. 'Thank you,' Grannie said. 'You seem like a nice young man.'

'Now, don't make too much noise down below tonight,' said Issie.

Agnes, Emma and Stephen went to the basement, where Emma's friends were waiting. They were Dicky, Donald and Ann. The carpet was already rolled back for dancing, and Stephen at once made himself popular by taking turns at winding the gramophone. The others sat on the edge of the bed, which had the merit of somewhat obscuring it.

Stephen was older than the others. Dicky was nineteen, handsome in his mother's Fair Isle knitted jumper and his spotless linen, changed by her every day. Ann was seventeen, and Donald eighteen. Stephen seemed to settle as comfortably with them as a good-humoured tabby cat which had just strayed into the house. He was complimentary to Agnes's inevitable bread pudding and drank his tea thirstily, though Emma thought he would have liked something stronger. She remembered the cocktails at Eric's. Somehow they all seemed to realise that he was Emma's property, and she felt proud. If only her mother would go away! Dicky sang and played the ukulele, and Agnes was prevailed upon to do a few steps of the *Cachuca* which she had once performed in *The Gondoliers*. They all asked her to do this, though Emma was embarrassed. She thought women of forty-five should at least keep quiet.

Yet she was grateful for her mother's tolerance of these Saturday evenings and only hoped she would let them have some beer to drink soon. She was afraid Stephen might be disappointed and would go away.

She need not have worried. Before the evening was out and Aunt Issie had made her grim ritual appearance with the clock, he had asked Agnes if he might take Emma to the Hammersmith Palais de Danse. This made Agnes apprehensive, as she knew she could not go with them.

'But you mustn't keep her late,' she said. 'She must be home by eleven.'

So Emma went, unchaperoned, and her delight was extreme. She told Stephen how nice it was that her mother was not with them. 'I know she means well,' she said, 'but she's terrified of letting me out of her sight.'

'She takes good care of you,' he answered, 'which is only natural since your father died.' His face was grave. 'She doesn't know that I should take good care of you, too.'

She loved his proprietorial air. Certainly she was in love, and this time for ever. They arrived home at twenty past eleven, to find Agnes standing by the open door, watching for them.

'Where have you been? I've been nearly out of my mind!'

'Oh, Mother, don't be so absurd! What could have happened to me? Our Tube broke down, and we were held up for a quarter of an hour.'

43

'I'm awfully sorry, Mrs Sheldrake,' said Stephen, 'but it was no fault of ours. I'm sorry you've been worried. Now you won't let me take her out again,' he added, but seductively.

'That will depend. Come on in, Emma. Say good-night to Stephen.'

When they were in the house Emma's temper overflowed.

'Mamma, how could you? Watching for us like that. I was ashamed.'

'You don't know how it is when you've got an only child. One hears of such things these days. . . .'

'You knew I'd be safe with Stephen.'

'But suppose you'd both had an accident?'

'Now, is that likely? You've quite spoiled my evening.'

'Don't be silly.' But Agnes added, 'I hope you had a good time. I ought to have been with you.'

'Could you have stopped the train from breaking down? And I'm quite old enough to go out with Stephen alone.'

In fact, next week was to be her sixteenth birthday. She was leaving school, despite the distress of the headmistress, who had wanted her to go to Oxford. 'I'm sure we could have got over the maths difficulty somehow.'

'But Emma must earn a living and be trained for something. If she ever marries and it doesn't turn out well, she will always have something at the back of her.'

Agnes was too concerned for Emma's future to be in as much awe of her headmistress as usual.

Emma was enrolled in a secretarial college off Bond Street. The fee for the six months' course was eighty pounds, which used up almost the whole of her mother's savings. It was a place mainly for smart girls who did not need jobs, but were training as an insurance. Emma was relieved to find that they were all required to wear flowered overalls, which blurred the distinctions between dress. Miss Serin had done much to live up to the occasion, but it was not fully within her powers.

Emma loved her morning journeys there. She took the number 19 bus from the nearby terminus to Bond Street, and then walked up it looking at the shops on her way. They educated her tastes, though she had not, nor ever expected to have, the money to satisfy them. She became an expert on hand-made underwear, slips and nightdresses of embroidered satin. From the picture dealers she soon learned which modern paintings were in fashion, and from the antique dealers to acquire a love of fine furniture. At lunch-time she went out with another impoverished girl called Nancy Steel to the ABC, where they ate poached eggs and chips and blackcurrant sponge pudding. At least, they ate like this when the money would stretch to it (Agnes allowed Emma ten shillings a week for fares, food and a packet of cigarettes; Emma had now become a smoker, though by necessity a very moderate one) and, when it would not, contented themselves with a bun and a glass of milk.

Emma was slow at the beginning with shorthand, but then it suddenly fell into place for her. She learned to touch-type rapidly, having used her mother's machine for some time. She was soon promoted to a course in French shorthand and in journalism, the latter not seeming to promise great usefulness. At book-keeping, according to form, she was very bad.

Meanwhile, she was engrossed in Stephen. She had been taken to meet his father – a tall, courteous man with hair *en brosse* of whom she was somewhat in awe – in a pub in Wimbledon, and later home to meet his mother, whom she found as welcoming as Sylvia. They asked her to bring her mother to see them shortly, and Agnes jumped at the chance. It would give her an opportunity to see if they were respectable, though she expected they would be, as Stephen's parents. The worst was anticipated by Aunt Issie, who blamed Agnes for allowing her daughter so much freedom.

The Saturday nights became fewer, since Stephen liked to take her out then, and Agnes would permit no other night. 'Remember, she has to get up early in the mornings.'

On Saturday afternoons, Stephen would take her to Wimbledon Common, where they lay in the woods above Queensmere. This Agnes hated and feared, for to her all young men were potential rapists, even the benign Stephen. She watched for them between the curtains when they were due back from these jaunts, though she did not again appear at the door.

Meanwhile Stephen, whom Aunt Issie had denounced suspiciously as a whited sepulchre, fondled and excited Emma, who was filled with delight and a sense of guilt, though he never exceeded this. It was understood that they should get married some day.

'Do you remember the paper ring I gave you at the dance?'

'I shall never forget.'

'I love you, you know.'

'And I love you.'

The trees seethed above their heads, and rays of sunlight filtered through. Children played hide and seek about them and went whooping with Indian cries down to the lake. Emma was serenely happy. He had driven away the fears from her mother's revelations, and she was sure she would enjoy sex when they were married. Not before, of course; that would be wrong and against the Commandments.

'When will your mother let us get engaged?' he asked.

'Not yet, I'm sure. But perhaps when I'm a working woman.'

He laughed. 'You a working woman! But I'm sure you'll be good at it. I shall give you a proper ring when you are. My grandmother left me one of hers, and I shall have it altered for you. It would be better than anything I can afford right now.'

The two households were drawing close together. Agnes and Emma went to tea with the Hoods, and saw Sylvia, who was very like her mother, and the young boy Noel. Then Mr and Mrs Hood came to tea with Agnes and met Grannie and Issie. It was the year of the General Strike, and Emma, who was quite unpolitical, found nothing but fun in having under-graduate bus drivers and conductors, and seeing office workers go to their places of business on the backs of lorries. It stupefied her to hear that Sylvia was on the side of the strikers. 'But they deserve more money, Emma. Look at it that way. Those undergraduates are just blacklegs.'

Sylvia herself, however, was obliged to accept lifts on lorries to the dress-shop where she worked. The Hoods lived in an old-fashioned large house in Balham, and her job was in the West End of London.

'Don't listen to Syl,' Stephen said. 'She's just an old red. I don't know where she gets it from.'

46

'And I'm a red, too,' said Noel.

'You speak when you're spoken to,' said Stephen, and they pushed each other about a bit.

'Is she Steve's latest?' Noel said in an audible whisper to Sylvia.

Stephen, who coloured easily, blushed up to his ears.

Emma was taken by an uprush of jealousy. Was that all she was, his 'latest'? She saw him as a Don Juan.

'Be quiet, little boy,' Sylvia said fondly, 'and stuff your mouth full of cake. Don't take him seriously, Emma; he's just growing too big for his boots.'

Emma's fears subsided somewhat.

She liked his family; she saw that her mother had taken to them and they to her. Agnes, now long out of mourning, was as pretty as ever. She had saved up enough money for Emma to have at last the desired permanent wave, which meant being strung up by the hair to a machine for three hours, but which became her and softened her rather austere features. Stephen had much approved.

Aunt Issie, however, had not. 'Look at the curled darling,' she had greeted her, quoting from something or other, and infuriating Emma. 'I liked it straight.'

'Well, I didn't,' Emma replied and fell into a long silence.

At the end of her course, the college found her a job in a small travel agency in Oxford Street. Her salary, to dignify it by that name, was two pounds a week, from which her mother let her retain twelve shillings. This meant that she always went hungry on Thursdays, and had a lunch-time orgy on Fridays, pay-days. It was a cheerful job, and she liked it. The head of the firm was a very tall man with five children. He called her 'Miss Sheldrake', which made her feel important. Though she was junior to Miss Grace, who worked mainly in the outer office, she soon found herself acting as secretary to Mr Blunt, who had discovered that it was actually sufficient to give her the gist of a reply to have her write the letter herself. She had no book-keeping to do but to take charge of the stamp-book, and this she found difficult enough. Soon she was allowed to write personal letters from Mr Blunt to acquaintances with whom he did not much want to be bothered, and achieved such proficiency in copying his style that she came to believe that she caused as much affront as pleasure. The number of personal letters dwindled. Miss Grace was her senior by about five years, pretty and competent. She soon began calling Emma by her first name and sometimes advanced her a shilling or two on Thursdays, when the thought of a bun and milk seemed too much to bear. Often Stephen, whose office closed half an hour earlier than Emma's, would call for her and take her home. He would come straight into the agency and wait for her, which made her very proud. All in all, life was very good.

Agnes continued to take in typing. She had some striking clients, including a Chinese who had written a play which was to be a success and, unforgettably, a Colonel Cody, who arrived wearing long moustaches and a great Stetson hat, who claimed to be the grandson of Buffalo Bill. Aunt Issie still worked in the auction rooms, and Grannie, deserted for a large part of the day, had to be content with her wireless set.

But Grannie was failing. She was by now totally blind, unable to see even the shapes of people, and she had more difficulty in finding her way about. 'It's no good,' Issie said. 'I shall have to give up my job and look after her.' Which is what happened, and made a diminution in the household income.

Emma invariably sang or played to Grannie in the evenings, except on Saturdays. She had learned several Negro spirituals, and Grannie loved and wept over 'Nobody Knows the Trouble I've Seen'. Emma was more patient with her than before, and always managed half an hour's reading. Even Issie was pleased with her.

Chapter Six

AT THE END of the year, Grannie died in her sleep. Agnes and Issie were at first beyond consolation, and the funeral arrangements were made by Emma. The wireless, with its earphones, fell into disuse since nobody else cared to listen to it. Emma sat with Grannie's corpse for an hour before the undertakers came, and was fascinated by the sight of death. Grannie, the colour of tallow, looked peaceful and asleep, her blind eyes closed. Emma regretted not having read to her more, and even more sharply that she had made jokes at Grannie's expense with her friends. But that was all over and no harm was done.

It soon became obvious that the house was now too large for them, even the two floors which they inhabited, and it was Aunt Issie's idea that they should sell it.

'But where shall we go?' said Agnes dolefully. She looked at Emma.

'I shall go and live with Marie, if she'll have me,' Issie said, referring to an old friend of hers, 'and you two had better see if you can get a couple of rooms in Chelsea. I know Emma's always hankered after living there. We can't go on like this, rattling about like peas in a pod. We'd better advertise at once.' She added, 'And you'll take Polly with you, of course. I don't think Marie would want her.'

'And I don't want that damned bird!' Emma said furiously. 'It's never done anything except try to bite me since I was born. I have to skirt the cage every time.'

'Don't use that language,' Issie said. 'You'll have to take Polly whether you like it or not.'

'Of course, she was always jealous of Emma, even when she was a baby,' Agnes protested timidly. 'It took the attention off her.'

'If only Reggie were here! He loved Polly. So did Mother. There's nobody left to love her now.'

Emma felt Issie was being mawkish about this ferocious African Grey, but she said nothing.

She and her mother were lucky in their hunt for rooms. They found, almost at once, four of them in a run-down house off the King's Road. There was a living-room of good size, with space for the sideboard and Emma's piano, two smallish bedrooms, and a kitchen with a bath concealed beneath the table. The lavatory was a floor down, but there was a sink on their landing.

Because they had sold the Rise house for a fairly good price, Agnes had been able to afford some redecoration, and to buy two beds. She knew Emma would welcome that relief. She brought the curtains from the basement room, and fitted them anew. She bought some new bed-linen.

Because the curtains were in autumn colours, she had the living-room repainted yellow. It all looked very cheerful and welcoming. She had taken the parrot into her own bedroom, where it slept all night under a baize cover and spent its days saying 'Kiss Mother, dear,' and 'Pretty Poll'. Emma, when making the beds, skirted the cage cautiously as usual. The Benin mask, taken from the high shelf, was proudly displayed on top of the piano, because Sylvia Hood had pronounced it beautiful.

They gave a flat-warming party for Stephen, Sylvia, and Emma's old friends. Issie had not wanted the gramophone. Dicky came, and Donald, and Ann and Silly Millie, who had grown so pretty and so affected that Emma was wary of her. But Stephen did not seem to be attracted.

This was liberation. She caught the same bus for work but did not have to be quite so early for it. The new address pleased her, and she was glad to give it to Mr Blunt, whom she thought it would please also.

The Saturday evenings now had the same bread pudding, but Agnes allowed a glass or two of beer, brought in by Dicky or Stephen. The room was not large enough for much dancing, but they turned back the carpet as usual. Stephen and Ann liked each other, but not in a way to cause Emma agitation.

Ann was now engaged, very well indeed, to a stockbroker, and brought him along one evening, but he was by far the oldest of the party and seemed embarrassed by it. After that, Ann, a girl of independent mind, came on her own. Dicky had conceived, inconveniently, a mooning kind of passion for Emma. She admired his spotlessness but could not respond, and Stephen did not appear to be perturbed. Occasionally he brought Sylvia, who fitted in well with the rest of the party.

Agnes was delighted with the success of the move. She missed Issie, who had gone to live with her friend, but was enchanted to be surrounded by youth and, she thought, trusted by them.

One Saturday evening, by way of experiment, she went to the cinema and did not return till about half-past ten. She did not receive quite the ecstatic welcome she expected, but was asked eagerly about the film.

'I'm mad about Sylvia Sydney,' said Ann. 'I must go, too.'

'We've no Aunt Issie now to bring in the clock,' Stephen said, 'so we may have overstayed our time.'

'Eleven is the deadline now,' said Emma. 'None of you need stir until then.'

On Sunday mornings, Agnes still insisted on taking her to St Mark's Church. 'I promised Mr Mossop that we wouldn't desert him.'

Emma did not care. She no longer tried to keep her mind on the sermon, but enjoyed the liturgy, the wholehearted hymn-singing and the anthem by the choir. Every Sunday she prayed to be made better, but so far as she could see there was no improvement. She prayed for her mother and for Stephen (whose religious faith seemed to be in some doubt), prayed to love Aunt Issie. She did not pray to love Polly: that was past praying for.

On her seventeenth birthday, Stephen asked Agnes if he and Emma might become engaged. Agnes was flustered. 'She's so young! What will your parents think?'

'I think they'd be pleased. Of course, we couldn't marry for a long time, not until I got promotion, and even then I dare say Emma would go on working.'

'But where would you live?'

'I expect she'd be very welcome in our house. It's large enough, and everyone's fond of her.'

'Well, I don't know. I can't answer now.'

When he had gone, she rounded on Emma. 'So you want to leave me!'

'Don't be ridiculous, Mother. We only want to be engaged. All those plans are for the distant future.'

'No. I shall be all alone. And I thought we should be so happy here.'

But, despite all this, Emma and Stephen did become engaged, with the blessing of his parents, Sylvia and even Noel, who was excited by the news. Stephen gave her his grandmother's ring, a fair-sized diamond on a broad gold band, which he had had narrowed for her. She showed it around the office with delight, and Mr Blunt said, from his great height, 'Congratulations, Miss Sheldrake. But you mustn't leave us yet awhile.'

'Oh, I shan't be able to. It will be some time before I can get married.'

She felt acutely the dignity of her new state. Now Ann was no longer the only engaged girl, though she would be marrying sooner. Silly Millie was openly envious, Don impassive, and Dicky moped. His ukulele lay idle. Since her engagement, some of the spirit had gone out of the Saturdays, and this made Emma sorry. She even felt that a part of her youth had passed away.

One day they invited Miss Plimsoll to tea. It was Emma's idea: it would save them that journey to Putney and show her what a real tea could be. To their surprise, she accepted, probably curious to know what their new home was like.

On a Saturday afternoon she mounted the stairs with some difficulty, complaining all the way. 'I don't know how you stand it, so high up, Emma. One flight's enough for me.'

She was wearing a grey hat with a bird on it. This she did not remove.

'This must have cost you a pretty penny,' she said, looking round the living-room. 'I'm sure I don't know how you manage it, Agnes. Do you still do typing? I don't see any machine.'

Agnes said she typed on the kitchen table.

'Get much work?'

'My old customers haven't deserted me.'

Miss Plimsoll was told that Emma was engaged, and was shown the ring.

'Far too young! You're just a child. Who's the man?'

'Stephen Hood. He works in a bank.'

'Then you won't be likely to have many pennies to bless yourselves with. When are you getting married? You'll be lonely,' she said to Agnes. 'Far too young to leave the nest.'

'We're not sure when it will be,' said Emma, but she was excited. She had had a pay-rise from the agency and was now earning two pounds ten shillings a week. She hoped to be promoted to Miss Grace's position; she also was to be married shortly.

'Well, if you both get into trouble, don't blame me for not telling you.'

Agnes brought in the tea, but even this did not please. 'And you're wasting the electric light. Much too early in the day to light up. Cucumber sandwiches? They give me indigestion.'

'Paste, then?'

'What kind?'

'Chicken-and-ham paste.'

'I'll just have one,' Miss Plimsoll said dubiously, and Emma realised that she and her mother would have to make a supper of sandwiches.

'Not brandy-snaps, please. They'll break my teeth. I'll just have a piece of plain cake. Pity you went to all this trouble for me. I'm simple in my tastes. – I don't see the parrot.'

'Polly's in my bedroom,' said Agnes. 'I always put her there when people come, because she's so noisy.' And, indeed, a faint 'Kiss Mother, dear,' sounded from a back room.

'Your grannie wouldn't have been pleased,' Miss Plimsoll said to Emma. 'She was devoted to that bird.'

'Unfortunately the bird wasn't devoted to me. She was always trying to bite.'

'Don't take me up so sharp, just because you're engaged and think you're grown-up.'

'I am grown-up, to all intents and purposes.'

'Emma hasn't improved,' Miss Plimsoll said to Agnes. 'You're spoiling her.'

'Who else have I got to spoil, since Reggie died?'

'You must miss him very much,' said Miss Plimsoll, softening a little. 'He was such a live wire. Extravagant, though.'

She added to Emma, 'When you do get married, don't trouble to ask me. I seldom go out. And, besides, I don't approve.'

Emma wanted to say, 'Nobody asked you to approve,' but she held her tongue.

'Do you see much of Issie?'

'She comes about once a fortnight. She's got another job near to where she lives,' said Agnes.

'She was always fond of Reggie,' said Miss Plimsoll, with uncommon perception. 'She must miss him more than anyone.'

This slur on her mother and herself aroused Emma, who said, 'Not more than we do.'

'Smart! I don't like smartness.'

'Emma didn't mean anything,' said Agnes, a trifle slavishly. She had always been a little in awe of Miss Plimsoll.

'I'd better go to the bathroom.'

Guessing what she meant, Agnes escorted her down a flight. 'How you can put up with this!' the guest exclaimed. 'I must have everything on one floor.'

'We had to take what we could get. And this had the biggest rooms.'

Miss Plimsoll disappeared into the lavatory, saying 'Don't wait for me. I like to take my time.'

'Has she said a pleasant thing all the afternoon?' Emma demanded, when Agnes returned.

'Sh, dear, she's getting very old and you can see that she's got rheumatism. If I'd thought about our stairs, I shouldn't have asked her.'

'And all those nice sandwiches wasted,' said Emma, immediately echoing her mother. 'But we'll have them for supper!'

'Be quiet, she's coming back.'

Miss Plimsoll seemed redder-faced than usual, and somewhat embarrassed. 'I couldn't get that flush to work.'

'Don't worry,' Emma said, 'I'll see to it.' She was glad to get out of the room for a few minutes.

When she came back, Agnes was helping Miss Plimsoll into her coat.

'I was telling your mother, I don't like to be late out now that the nights are drawing in.'

'I'll see you out,' Emma said, and was complimented on her strong young legs.

Miss Plimsoll thanked them both in a perfunctory way and took her leave.

'A pity she couldn't stay to see Stephen,' Agnes said.

'I don't think it's a bit of a pity. She'd only have been rude to him.'

'But he would have been very nice to her.'

'She doesn't deserve people being nice to her.'

'Don't be hard, darling. People get queer when they've been alone as much as she has. I dare say her heart's in the right place.'

'She hasn't got a heart to be in any place.'

'Shall we bring Polly in now? I don't like to think of her all alone in the bedroom.'

'If you must, you must,' replied Emma.

Stephen came with a proposition. 'But I don't know what you'll think of it,' he said to Emma, when they were alone. 'I was wondering if, when we got married, I could move in with you until we could afford something of our own. I could easily pay my way. And she wouldn't have to miss you so horribly. My mother's got my father, and Syl and Noel, so it wouldn't be the same for her.'

Emma was taken aback. She had never dreamed of anything like this. She did not, however, doubt her mother's delight. 'I'll sound her out,' she said, 'but you would feel horribly cramped.'

'As if I'd mind being cramped with you! Besides, perhaps it would mean us getting married rather earlier.'

Agnes, when this plan was revealed to her later, was both appalled and overjoyed. 'Well, I dare say we could get another bed into Emma's room but, Stephen, how would you manage with a bath under the kitchen table? Yours is such a big house.'

'I could take my turn. Honestly, Mrs Sheldrake, I've thought it all out. It's only a matter for your approval and whether you could cope with another person.'

'Have you mentioned this to your parents?'

'Just about. But they let me go my own way. Emma and I could get married in December then.'

Negotiations between the two households went on. Mr Hood was dubious; Mrs Hood was willing that everything should be made easy for the young people. They came to tea with Agnes when Emma was at work, and there was a conclave.

'But he'll never settle here!' Agnes said. 'He's used to so much better.'

'He can adapt himself,' said Mrs Hood. 'Of course we should be delighted if Emma came to us, but Stephen seems keen on the other plan. They'll soon be earning enough between them to look for a larger flat, which would be big enough for you all.'

Agnes, transported by pleasure at this idea of having Emma indefinitely to herself, took care not to betray it.

So it was planned, and the arrangements for the wedding went ahead. It was not to be a full-white affair, which Agnes, even with the Hoods' assistance, could not afford, but neither was it to be in a registry office, which was desired neither by herself nor by her daughter. It was to be held in St Mark's Church, with only relations present. Emma was to wear a short white dress and a white hat. The week's honeymoon was to be spent alone at Eric Flowers' bungalow, which he would have properly aired and dried out for them, and stocked with food. 'December's not good for the river,' he wrote to them, 'but you have my word that it will be all right for you both.'

But a fortnight before the date fixed for the marriage, Emma received an ugly shock. This came in the form of a postcard enclosed in an envelope with the address printed; it had not excited Agnes so much that she had kept it from Emma.

The contents were printed, too, in bright blue ink.

SO YOU'VE CAUGHT A MAN HA HA HA YOU AND YOUR GIDDY
MAMMA GOD HELP HIM. EMMA LET THE POOR BLEEDER GO
BEFORE IT'S TOO LATE. I KNOW ALL ABOUT YOU I WATCH YOU
WHEREVER YOU GO. YOU THINK YOU'RE SO SUPERIOR TO YOUR
FRIENDS WHEN I KNOW WHAT YOU GET UP TO. HA HA HA.

Emma had only just read this when she burst into tears.
Agnes took the card from her.

'I can't get married, Mother. I must be red with sin.'

'What on earth can you mean, darling?' Agnes saw that her
daughter was on the verge of hysteria. 'You've committed no
sins.'

But Emma, who had sometimes masturbated despite warn-
ings of blindness and insanity, could not stop crying. 'I must
be wicked if somebody hates me so.'

'Don't talk nonsense. I know you as I know myself.' (This
was not quite true.)

'Who on earth could have sent it? It is somebody who
watches all we do. That's the horrible part. It couldn't be Miss
Plimsoll?'

'How absurd! She's too old. She's nearly eighty.'

'But who? Oh, what shall I do?'

'Tear it up and forget it. And do stop crying. You're doing
just what the writer hopes,' said Agnes.

Emma gave the card into her hand, but Agnes, though she
went into the kitchen ostensibly to do so, did not destroy it.
She fancied there would a follow-up and, if so, they could go
to the police. She hid the repulsive thing with a shudder
beneath her own mattress.

'Don't tell Stephen,' Emma said when she came back. 'It's
too horrible.'

'I wouldn't dream of it.'

'But I can't marry him now.'

'Don't talk such nonsense. And of course I shouldn't tell
him.'

For the rest of the day they debated who could have been the
sender, and every one of their friends fell under suspicion. It
seemed that Emma would never again see anyone as completely innocent. She went to bed red-eyed and exhausted.

57

She and Stephen were, however, married at the end of the
year. The wedding was at St Mark's, conducted by Mr
Mossop, and the expenses were shared by Agnes and the
Hoods. Mr Hood had only his retirement pension, but his wife
had a little money of her own. Stephen was in a dark suit with a
rose in his buttonhole; Emma, as planned, in white. She was in
the deep happiness of a dream. They all went back to the flat,
where champagne was waiting for them, and a buffet breakfast, organised by Issie's friend Marie, was laid out on the big
sideboard. Agnes had not shed the traditional tears as the
bride's mother, but Issie had openly wept. 'So young, so
young,' she kept saying. She was the first to call Emma 'Mrs
Hood'. Agnes did not cry, because she had something else on
her mind. That morning she had intercepted another postcard – an open one this time – addressed to Emma and had
hidden it with the other one.

SO YOU'RE A MARRIED LADY HA HA HA WON'T YOU SWANK
THOUGH YOU'VE NOTHING TO SWANK ABOUT AS YOU'RE NO
BEAUTY THAT GIDDY MOTHER MUTTON DRESSED UP AS LAMB
WON'T KNOW HER ARSE FROM HER ELBOW. MAY YOU BOTH GET
WHAT YOU DESERVE WHICH ISN'T MUCH I SHALL BE WATCHING
YOU.

This almost, but not quite, poisoned the day for her,
though, as the champagne took hold, she felt better. She was
lucky not to be losing Emma after all.
    Sylvia hugged her new sister-in-law with unfeigned de-
light. 'You look quite beautiful! Doesn't she, Steve?'
    'Entirely beautiful,' he said gravely.
    Emma looked forward without fear to the night. Her sexual
longing had become so acute that she had long dreamed of its
satisfaction, though Agnes had told her nervously that she
mustn't expect pleasure all at once. It was Stephen who was
the more nervous.
    She was glad when the time came for them to take the taxi to
the station. She had changed into a blue suit and had put the
white one away for some more delicate occasion.
    The wedding party saw them off from the doorstep, throw-

ing confetti and rose-petals. 'Someone will have to sweep that up,' Issie commented. But she kissed Emma and Stephen and wished them luck.

They arrived at the bungalow before dusk. To their pleasure, Eric had left the lanterns lit, had prepared supper for them and put hot-water bottles in the beds. He left a note that the daily woman would be coming regularly to help out.

It was a mild night, the moon reflected in the river.

'Do you remember—?' Stephen began.

'Of course I remember! I shall never forget. Hasn't Eric been good to us?' Besides all this, he had given them a handsome wedding present, a Waterford flower-bowl.

'Let's dance,' said Stephen when they had eaten, 'just for old times' sake.' So they wound up the gramophone and moved together over the deserted veranda, under the lantern.

They sat up rather late, neither liking to be the first to suggest that they went to bed. It was Emma who took the initiative. 'I suppose I'd better put the lanterns out. We'll light them again tomorrow night.'

'I can't think beyond tonight,' said Stephen, and slipped his tongue between her lips. He had never kissed her so before, and it excited her still further. She undressed in the larger of the two bedrooms and waited for him to come to her.

When he did, he tried to take her at once, but failed. 'I'm sorry, darling. It will be better next time.'

Emma, disappointed, cried herself to sleep but in a couple of hours was awakened by him. He was naked and erect. Without a word he took her again and, still gently, broke the hymen. It was painful but it was wonderful. True pleasure would have to come, however, later. He did not leave her bed but settled himself at her side, and went to sleep at once.

Chapter Seven

AFTER A WEEK of sexual and romantic bliss, they returned to the flat. Agnes welcomed them this time, rather tearfully. She had made all arrangements for their return, placing in Emma's room a new divan bed for two people. This she had bought in part-exchange.

They were a proud couple now, aware of their married status. There was a week to go before Christmas, which they were to spend with the Hoods, and they both returned to their respective offices in the meantime. Emma was enthralled to hear herself addressed by her employer in her married name. She had declined to be called 'Miss Sheldrake'. Miss Grace's marriage had been delayed until March and, like her as she did, Emma would be pleased to see her go.

At home, Agnes cooked the evening meal and Emma and Stephen washed up. Everything they did together was a pleasure to them, or at least to Agnes.

But one Sunday morning Emma, doing the bedrooms, decided to turn her mother's mattress and the two postcards were revealed. She read the second of them with horror, knowing that her mother had resolved to hide them. So she went to Stephen.

He was appalled. He asked, of course, who could have sent them. To which there was no answer. Agnes was angry that Emma had shown them to him. 'It's our affair. There's no reason for him to be worried.'

'I'm not worried,' he said. 'I'm simply horrified. I suggest that you wait for another one and then tell the police.'

'What can they do?' Agnes asked. 'Except confirm that it's a woman. We're both sure of that.'

But for some time the cards ceased to come. The next came on New Year's Day and was addressed to Agnes.

SO YOU'VE GOT THEM BOTH CAGED HAVEN'T YOU GOT YOUR
LITTLE GIRL WELL IN SIGHT FOR EVER BECAUSE DON'T THINK
YOU'LL EVER LET THEM GO HA HA HA MAKE THE BEST OF WHAT
YOU'VE GOT GIDDY AGNES BECAUSE IT WON'T LAST LONG YOUR
WELLWISHER.

'How could you have kept these from me?' Stephen asked
Emma. 'They must have worried you out of your mind.'

'I did wonder', she said, 'what I could have done to be hated
so. I couldn't bear to show you.'

'People like this', he said wisely, 'get their pleasure from
writing this stuff and then dropping it in the post-box. That's
all.'

'But it's beastly to know that somebody knows all about
you.'

'We shall go to the police right away,' he said.

The police were not much good. A graphologist had confirmed that the writer was a middle-aged woman, but that was
all. The three cards disappeared into the police archives.

'What have I done to be hated so?' Emma reiterated to
Stephen one night.

'Nothing, darling. You mustn't let this prey on your mind.'

In the meantime, the Saturday evenings were resumed.
Ann, now married, brought her new husband, appreciably
older than any of Emma's friends. Dicky had stopped sulk-
ing. Don arrived, bringing an Everyman edition of Chaucer
as a belated wedding-present. Ann sent a toast-rack, Silly
Millie and her mother some salad-servers, and Miss Grace
some apostle spoons. 'How kind everyone is!' Emma exclaimed, and her mother said, 'Now you can see how they all
hate you.' She explained to Stephen, 'She didn't want to get
married at first. She thought she must be wicked if people
hated her so.'

'Mother!' Emma protested. 'I don't know how you can.'

'It was only to show you how stupid you've been.'

Stephen felt her embarrassment, smiled, and said nothing.
This was one of the times when Agnes grated on him.

At the beginning of January, Stephen had an inspiration. He
answered an advertisement in the paper from a large and

61

glossy motor-car firm in Piccadilly. It required a salesman, public-school man, aged 23/30, clean licence, able to service a car, personable, well spoken. Previous sales experience preferred but not essential. The money was half as much again as he made at the bank. Stephen was not too hopeful. He had driven the family car until his father sold it the previous year and was well able to cope with the mechanics of it, but had driven nothing else except, occasionally, Sylvia's Austin 7. But he was asked for an interview and went wearing his dark wedding-suit, having in a moment of pure panache and superstition put a flower in his buttonhole. To his amazement he was given the job. He returned home in a state of high excitement and waltzed Agnes round the kitchen. 'Now we shall be able to move to a larger flat! I'm going to ring Emma up and tell her, and be damned to them if they do mind private calls.'

She kissed him and made him drink a glass of sherry. 'It was that flower that did it,' she said. 'I was afraid it might put them off.'

Emma was wild with pleasure. Now they would be able to move to a flat in which the bathroom was separate from the kitchen table, and she would be able to take the same bus as he to work every day. She had always felt the cold and had hated the long chilly journeys on the top of the bus, where she sat envying and detesting the old men warm in their clubs, eating kidneys and bacon, or something as delectable. (The fact that she did not like kidneys seemed to make no difference.) Stephen had laid out some of his savings on a new overcoat and looked very smart. She was not surprised that he had been chosen. The work was a six-day week, with alternate Saturdays free. He told her he had beaten men from Rugby and Shrewsbury, and she was proud of him.

They set out flat-hunting on his first free Saturday, which she herself had been allowed to take off, and walked until they were tired. Everything they saw seemed too large, too sordid, too inconvenient and too dear. At last, at the end of the day – they had not stopped to eat – they came across a five-roomed flat at the other end of the King's Road, self-contained, at a rent of three pounds a week, which they could now afford to pay. They went back to the letting agency and made an offer. 'We shall have to have a week's rent down,' they were told, and Stephen was proud to pay it.

Their new home had been freshly painted, in white flushed with pink. There was a big bedroom for them to share (the previous one had been rather cramped), a bedroom for Agnes, and a smaller room they meant to call 'the study'. The lavatory was in the bathroom, which, too, was spick and span. 'It looks like Heaven to me,' said Emma.

They lost no time. In a fortnight they had moved in, and the Hoods had come to admire. 'I say, old boy,' said Sylvia, 'you do fall on your big feet.'

Money being less tight, they bought a Frigidaire on the hire-purchase system, and Agnes amused herself making ice-cream in it. It was agreed that the study should be hers, for her typewriting. She bought and made new curtains from a sea-green slub, and adapted the old ones for the bedroom windows. It was a first-floor flat, and there was not so far for her clients to climb. 'Let's hope Miss Plimsoll doesn't take a fancy to it,' said Emma. 'That would be more than I could bear.'

But she was thinking that there would now be room for a baby. She and Stephen had decided against having children for a while but, though their precautions had been perfunctory, there was no sign of a child as yet. Whether they would be able to afford one she did not know. It would mean her leaving her job for several months, and leaving the burden of support on Stephen and Agnes. So she let events take their course. The Saturday evenings began again. Dicky was now engaged and brought his girl, a beautiful red-head called Lucy. He seemed quite to have got over Emma. Ann came with her husband and sometimes Sylvia, too. As before, they danced to the gramophone. Agnes was not too willing to dance now, thinking herself too old; but she could not resist the invitation. After all, it was something she did well. She was graceful and light on her feet, and had profited by the lessons from poor Leslie.

Even Miss Grace, now Mrs Caldwell, married, but, to Emma's disappointment, not having surrendered her job as promised, came with her husband and was loud in approbation. 'You are lucky, Emma,' she said. 'Our flat is just a hutch to this one.' She said how well their employer's wedding-present, a gilt sunray clock, looked on the wall. 'He did you well, Emma, but mine be part of the praise, because I chose it.'

The felicity of Emma and Stephen was complete. He had succeeded, during his first month, in selling a Bentley to a rich man who already had a yacht, and had received a commission. On the strength of this he took Emma to Hatchett's, a smart restaurant off Piccadilly, and bought her a new dress for the occasion. She bought him a new tie, as her part of the celebrations. (Agnes had been asked but, tactfully, had not accepted. 'You don't want your mother-in-law round your neck the whole time,' she had said to Stephen, who had protested, but she spoke more truly than she knew. He was indeed fond of her, but had often wished that he and Emma could have an evening to themselves occasionally, even though Agnes usually retreated to the study with her typing.)

One night he said to Emma, 'I think your period's overdue.' He was nothing if not observant.

'Oh, are you sure? I didn't notice. It can't be over a few days, in any case.'

'A full week.'

'Well, that's not much.'

'I can't help watching out.'

'Would you be pleased?' she asked nervously.

'I think so, yes. We could just about manage it. When will you know?'

'Another week or ten days. Oh dear, now you've upset me.'

He kissed her. 'Nothing to get upset about. I dare say I should be just like a dog with two tails.'

When ten days had passed, Emma went to the doctor. He said that pregnancy was likely, but that she must give him a urine specimen which would be sent to the laboratory. In two days' time he telephoned her. The result was positive. He would like her to come and see him again.

Emma told her news to Agnes when Stephen was out. To her amazement she began to cry angrily. 'You've known all this time and never confided in me!'

'I wanted to be certain.'

'Then I've failed. I always knew it.'

'You always said it, Mother, so don't say it again. Aren't you pleased for me?'

'You're so young.'

'The younger the better, they say. Come on, now, stop crying. This isn't a tragedy. It's a cause for celebration.'

'I've brought you up to trust me, and this is what happens! A conspiracy of silence.'

'Well, you know now. And for sure, before Stephen. Stop it, Mother! I can't bear scenes. You know I can't. We both love you, but we can't bear them.'

There was a long pause, during which Agnes meticulously wiped her face. She said at last, 'It had better have the study for a nursery.'

'Too far down the passage. There's room for a cot in our bedroom. Look here, don't we have a drink to celebrate?'

'You're probably better off without it. And certainly better off not smoking.'

Emma lit another cigarette. She asked coaxingly, 'Would you like a boy or a girl?'

'I shouldn't care, so long as it was healthy.'

'What are we having for dinner tonight?'

'Why? I've made a steak-and-kidney pudding.'

'But we must have a glass of wine with it. We must do something special. I'll run over to the off-licence and get one.'

'My little girl a mother,' said Agnes maddeningly.

'If you'd said "My little girl a murderer" you couldn't have sounded more glum.'

'It was the shock of being told like that. What would your father have said?'

'He'd have cheered and sent out for some whisky.'

'Poor Reggie. I wonder.'

'Now, don't start that again and, above all, don't do it before Stephen. I must go and get that wine now.'

'You'll find a pound under the tea-caddy.'

But when Stephen did come home, and was told the news, Agnes had pulled herself together.

'My darling,' Stephen said, and kissed Emma on the lips. He could scarcely wait till they had an opportunity to be alone.

'I've been hoping for this, though I didn't dare to tell you.'

'Mother was bitter with me for keeping it from her for so long – the suspicion, I mean.'

'Your mother must master herself,' he said quaintly. 'This is our joy. And I don't care whether it's a boy or a girl so long as you're safe. But we must find names for both alternatives, because it looks so cold in the papers just to say "a daughter" or "a son".'

They caressed each other and discussed names until it was time for supper. By then, Agnes had completely recovered herself and was prepared to join in congratulation. They moved joyfully to practical things: whether Emma's and Stephen's bedroom could really contain a cot, where she should have the child, at home or in a hospital. 'I should like to have it at home,' Emma said, 'but Dr Finch thinks a hospital is always better. In case something should go wrong.'

'But what could go wrong?' Agnes cried. 'I had you at home.'

'Oh, nothing. But I shall take his opinion.'

'Any opinion but mine,' said Agnes, with a touch of her old acerbity. 'I'm the last to count.'

'Oh, Mother . . . have some more wine. We're going to be gay tonight.'

'I wish I'd thought to get flowers for the table.'

'That's better! I knew you'd rejoice really,' said Emma.

But she was not altogether blind to her mother's fierce feelings. A child the more would be a child the less.

Chapter Eight

Emma's employer was kind, and offered her six weeks' leave of absence before and after the birth of the child. He also, being remorseful about not implementing his promise to promote her when Miss Grace married, raised her salary to three pounds a week, which seemed like wealth to her.

The Hoods, especially Sylvia and Noel, were excited about her pregnancy. 'I shall be a very young uncle,' Noel said. Agnes was reconciled to the whole thing, though she still continued to complain that she had not been first confided in. 'You know how precious everything you do is to me,' she said to Emma. They went now on Sundays to Chelsea Old Church, since she thought the journey to St Mark's would be too much for her daughter. For the first month after conception Emma and Stephen did not have intercourse, but after that returned to it with relief. Agnes guessed at their sensuality and could not understand it. With Reggie, this had occurred about every three weeks, and had not been much welcomed by her when it did. Sometimes she even found herself calling Stephen 'animal' in her own mind. Everything alien to Agnes was quite Alien. Meanwhile, Emma was so eager for her pregnancy to be visible that she went into maternity dresses long before she needed to do so. Stephen was entranced when the baby made its first movements and loved to feel it within the wall of her stomach.

'I shall be a most indulgent papa,' he said, in his gentle voice. Whenever he made a sale he bought her presents: a recording of Ravel's 'Bolero', which had had its first performance that year; sweets, for which she had developed a craving now that she had cut down her smoking; and often flowers, which he would also buy for Agnes. He thought how lucky it was that he was fond of his mother-in-law, for now, especially, there would be no chance of leaving her. She would be more than useful when the baby came.

It was agreed that Emma should have it in hospital, since there would be no room in the flat for a nurse during the necessary weeks and, anyway, they could not afford one. One mild night in September, Emma's waters broke and Stephen himself took her in. He had a small car of his own now, bought at a discount from his firm. She was excited but unperturbed; she had had her bag packed for the last fortnight. A cot stood in the corner of their room with a screen round it, which Agnes had made out of a whitewood frame and some flowered cretonne.

When Stephen had at last to leave Emma in the maternity ward her pains had just begun, but she did not let him know this. 'You go along, my dear darling, and don't worry. Everything is going to be all right for us,' she said.

The birth was sharp but rapid. She did not cry out, but contented herself with a dog-like panting which, said the doctor, was the best thing she could do. She was mercifully given an anaesthetic during the final stages, and when she woke up was told that she had a boy.

'Is he all right?'

'He's fine. I'll ring up and tell your husband.'

It was six in the morning.

The baby, now washed and dressed, and having had his first statutory cry, was given to his mother. Immediately she felt an uprush of love. He was not very big, but he had even now a pronounced resemblance to Stephen. 'We shall call you Paul,' she said to him. She fell into a doze. When she awoke she found Stephen by her bed. It was eleven o'clock. The nurse brought the baby back and he was allowed to hold him. 'He's wonderful,' he said, 'and so are you.' Paul was put to Emma's breast, and she made her first attempt at feeding him. This Stephen watched with the stupefied rapture of one of the shepherds at the manger. 'He seems very strong,' she said. She added, 'When is Mother coming?'

He replied with unaccustomed firmness. 'I asked her to come at twelve. She wanted to come with me, but I told her a father had first rights. I'm afraid she was a bit hurt, though.'

'Poor Mamma, she would be. But I'm sure she'll understand. You were quite right to come first.'

But, when she did come, Agnes did not speak of her hurt.
She was all anxiety for Emma. 'How are you, darling? Was it
very dreadful?'

'No. I'd go through it again.'

'I hope that won't be for some time. I couldn't sleep a wink.
I kept on thinking about you and following you in my mind.
Thank God it's all over.' She, too, was allowed to hold Paul,
though she did so less naturally than Stephen had done. 'He's a
beautiful baby,' she said. 'Just think, now I'm a grandmother!
It makes me feel very old.'

Well, you're not very young, Emma thought.

'I'm afraid the patient must lie down again now, Mrs
Sheldrake,' said the nurse. 'You can see her again this
evening.'

Flowers arrived, from Stephen, her employer and Miss
Grace, the Hoods, who were to come in on the following day,
and from Stephen's boss. 'I feel just like a film star,' she said.

She was bitterly disappointed when a week had gone by to
find that she would not be able to feed Paul herself. She had so
little milk and he tugged at her for a mere quarter of an ounce
a feed. She felt the deprivation of the sensual pleasure of
suckling and the joy of having the baby close to her. Meanwhile the nurses mixed the bottles and brought them to her.
'You weren't meant to be a good cow, dear,' said one of
them.

By the time of her return home, she had learned to bath the
baby herself, to mix his feeds, and how to prepare the 6 a.m.
bottle so that it only needed reheating. Fortunately, Paul
proved a serene baby, content with his bottle, crying little and
sleeping well. He let Stephen and Emma have their own sleep
between 11 p.m. and six in the morning.

However, Emma was taking Stilboestrol to take away the
remainder of her milk, and this threw her into a deadly depres-
sion that she had somehow to conceal from Stephen. She did
not conceal it from Agnes. 'It's not uncommon, the first weeks
after birth,' said her mother. 'I know I had it with you.'

She was sharing the work of the baby, the mixing of bottles, the occasional feed, the evening bath. 'I can take over when you go back to work.'

'I shan't be able to go back yet awhile. I couldn't face it.'

'When Mr Blunt has been so kind—'

'Damn Mr Blunt,' said Emma.

But she did go back, and felt the better for it, worried only about the additional burden she had laid on Agnes, who was still struggling on with her typing. They had an occasional Saturday night, bringing Paul, in a carry-cot, into the sitting-room. They were accustoming him to noise and movement, and there was no tiptoeing round the cot. He would usually sleep serenely through the evening's entertainment, and if he did start to cry was taken back to the bedroom. He was much admired by all her friends, and she and Stephen felt very proud.

When Emma returned to work at the agency, the labour fell heavily upon Agnes, though they had now employed a cleaner for two hours a day. This was a kind woman with a great love for Paul. When she had washed up the breakfast things and cleaned the flat she would offer to wash his napkins before she left.

'You are very good, Mamma,' Emma said.

'I'm only glad to be some use at last.'

This fishing for compliments was only an irritation. Emma loved her mother, but could not bring herself to gratify her. Besides, she had only just paid her a compliment and that would have to do. There had been this awkwardness between them ever since she was fourteen, though she had tried to overcome it. She was conscious sometimes of giving pain, and would try to make up for it by the gift of chocolates or a bunch of violets.

Paul grew and prospered. He was a forward baby. At eight months he had said his first words, at ten months he had taken his first steps, tottering between Emma and Stephen cross-legged on the carpet, and uttering great cries of pleasure when he succeeded in getting from one to the other. His first reddish hair had fluffed away on the pillow.

This was the year of the great New York Stock Exchange crash. The agency was besieged by American clients seeking advice, reassurance, or both, and Emma was run off her feet.

Her father-in-law had lost his few American holdings and was hard pressed for money. Sylvia contributed to the household expenses and Noel, nothing if not active, had taken on a paper-round before school – this, much to his parents' dismay. 'There's something in not being lumbered with stocks and shares,' Agnes said to Emma. 'Fancy all those stockbrokers throwing themselves from skyscrapers!'

The same thought was echoed by Miss Plimsoll, who had invited herself round one Sunday to see the baby – 'I didn't come before because I don't like them at the bawling stage.' Issie was there, too, these days a rare visitor. She had found a job with an estate agent in north London.

They watched while Emma spooned sieved prunes and custard into Paul's hungry mouth. 'I hope he eats everything,' said Miss Plimsoll.

'He can't bear carrots. He simply spits them out.'

'Oh, I should never put up with that! You should try him again and again until he changes his mind.'

'I don't agree with forcing them.'

'Then you must. There's too little food going around the world today.'

'Waste of good carrots,' said Emma impudently, but Miss Plimsoll did not see the joke.

'I think we must leave it to his mother to know best,' said Issie rather unexpectedly. She was not given to standing up for her niece, but Miss Plimsoll's certainties annoyed her.

'Anyway, he eats like a horse,' said Stephen soothingly. They all admired Paul as he drank from a cup.

'Does he give you good nights?' said Miss Plimsoll, as if hoping for something with which to find fault.

Stephen replied that he was wonderful; he slept from eleven till 6 a.m.

Agnes came in with the tea-tray. 'Here, let me carry that,' said Stephen.

'I hope those aren't cucumber sandwiches,' said Miss Plimsoll. 'Cucumber always repeats.'

'They're egg,' Agnes assured her. 'I thought that wouldn't hurt you.'

'Well, I'll just have one.'

71

Issie made a hearty meal. She lived frugally at home. Her friend was a vegetarian, and Issie thought longingly sometimes of her mother's roasts and raised pies. She would go into an ABC in her lunch-hour and have a surreptitious sausage roll; her friend believed her converted to meatlessness, and she would not for the world disappoint her.

Again they discussed the Stock Exchange crash. 'All those men killing themselves,' said Miss Plimsoll. 'Don't they know it's a mortal sin?'

'I don't expect they were in the frame of mind to think of that,' said Emma.

'Now, now, don't make a jest of it!'

'I wasn't.'

'Poor chaps,' said Stephen, 'with their life-savings gone.'

'Comes of putting all your eggs in one basket.'

'Their eggs were in a good many baskets, you know.'

Miss Plimsoll did not care for Stephen to stand up to her. 'All your eggs in one basket,' she persisted.

'Have some orange cake,' said Agnes. 'It's home-made.'

'It will be too strongly flavoured. I have to take care of my stomach. I suppose you haven't a biscuit?'

'Stephen, be a dear and get some out of the kitchen cupboard. They're in the blue tin.'

'If it's not any trouble,' said Miss Plimsoll grudgingly.

'This is an excellent cake, Agnes,' Issie said. 'As good as Mother's was.'

'Your mother did far too much cooking until her sight failed. I never saw such a larder as hers.'

'Those were the days,' said Emma.

'You could hardly remember. Don't be so silly.'

'Come, I'm not so young as all that.'

'If I say you're young, you're young.'

'Old enough to be a mother,' said Issie, taking another piece of cake.

As she rose to go at last, Miss Plimsoll asked for another look at Paul. He was in the carry-cot, playing with his teddy-bear. 'I like children,' she said unexpectedly. 'Some children.' She allowed him to curl his fingers round one of hers. 'You've got quite a grip, young man,' she told him.

'Don't you think she's softening with the years?' Issie suggested when she had gone.

'She's softened to Paul,' said Emma. 'That's all she does soften to.'

When Issie had gone and Agnes had returned to her typing – Emma and Stephen would do the washing-up later – Emma said, 'I am so happy. I feel I've everything in the world I need.'

'So do I,' he answered, 'but we could do with just a bit more money. I don't like to see Agnes slaving away like that.' He called his mother-in-law now by her Christian name.

'Time for baby's bath. Are you coming to watch?'

'Am I! I don't get much chance. Does he like his rubber duck?'

They rejoiced in his splashings, in his mottled legs, his jolly smile. His nose, they thought, was just like his father's.

When they had settled him for the night Stephen said, 'Quick, darling, I want you.'

The clicking of the typewriter sounded through the wall.

Chapter Nine

THEY took their holidays in the last week of September and the first week of October. This eccentric arrangement was due to a change in his plans of Miss Grace's husband, who was to have taken them both away on 1 September, for which Emma had originally made her arrangements, but of course in this matter Miss Grace had priority. Emma got Stephen to take his holiday at the same time as hers; they would not be going away, but at least they would be spending their time together. They insisted on sending Agnes to a Brighton hotel for a week's rest. At first she resisted this hotly, saying that they could not afford it, that she was not in the least tired, that she might lose good clients, that they could never get on without her. But Stephen had recently made a commission on a sale and he and Emma were adamant. They would not be tied to the house, because Sylvia was coming in twice to mind the baby, and they could go to the pictures or perhaps to a theatre. They had not been to a theatre for years.

'So you've been making your plans without telling me!'

'If we'd told you,' said Emma, 'you'd only have made more of a fuss. You must take your evening dress, by the way. There's dancing after dinner.'

'I shall look hopelessly shabby.'

'No, you won't,' Stephen assured her. 'You'll look very nice. And it's not really a smart place.'

'And I shall be so far away from you, if anything happened!'

'Sixty minutes from London.'

'And half an hour to get to the station, and half an hour to get back!'

'Now, Mother, nothing's going to happen,' said Emma. 'You go and really put your feet up. The weather won't matter.'

When she had gone, still fearing the worst, they were at first light-headed at the thought of being alone. Feeling disloyal, they waltzed together round the sitting-room, in which they had now installed a play-pen. Paul was able to haul himself to his feet and play with the small abacus that was set into it. He now wore knickers and smocks.

'I shall write to you' had been Agnes's last words.

She was as good as her word. She wrote to them on the second day, and her letter was far better than might have been expected.

Dearest Emma and Stephen,

You were probably right that I needed a rest. It is very pleasant here, though I dread to think how much it is costing you. I have taken a walk along the front and have been as far as Hove.

Last night you would not have known me. Greatly daring, I thought I would go in for the dancing. It is a small floor, but there is a good little band. My dress didn't look so bad; they aren't very dressy here. There is a professional who asked me to dance. He said I was very good and seemed surprised. No wonder, at my age! Then I was asked by a guest, an elderly man with a crippled wife, who invited me to their table afterwards and gave me a gin and it. I didn't stay long. And then, believe it or not, I was asked by a really *young* man, who danced divinely and complimented me. Then he sat down with me, and we had another drink. (You can see that I am going it!) We had quite a long talk. I think he is 'one of *those*'. He keeps an antique shop in the Lanes. He has lost his mother, and lives with an older friend called Robert, of whom he seems very fond. I went up to bed shortly after that and slept like a log.

Despite all these gaieties, I miss you and never stop thinking of you both and the darling baby.

'So you see,' Emma said to Stephen, 'it is a raging success.'

They cherished every moment of their week together. They went twice to the cinema (once, experimentally, they took Paul, who slept through most of the film and made little fuss

75

when he woke up) and once to *Bitter-Sweet*. Sylvia did not mind them being late as she had her small car, and had no trouble whatsoever with Paul, who blithely accepted his bed-time meal and bath at her hands. 'I must have one of these of my own, sometime, sweetie,' she said to Emma.

Emma cooked all Stephen's favourite dishes, starchier than Agnes approved, and they made love at random times. They were very content, and hard put to it to conceal this fact when Agnes came home.

'Well, now it's your turn to get some rest,' she told them, when she had taken off her hat and coat. 'You can't have had much.'

'Sylvia's been very good.'

'You won't need Sylvia now. You can go out every night, if you like. Did you remember to feed Polly?'

'She wouldn't let us forget her.'

'She hasn't been in my bedroom all that time?'

'I didn't want her in the sitting-room with baby.'

They heard Agnes making sympathetic cooing noises to the bird.

Emma did the cooking during the final week of their holiday and Agnes the shopping. She said it did her good to get out. She had become used to fresh air. She was quite eager to talk about her experiences at the hotel, and told them much about Mr Lawrence, the antique dealer, and the man with the crippled wife. 'So sad for him, though you can see she doesn't grudge him his pleasures. And he takes her in a chair every day along the Palace Pier. They're residents, you know. It must cost them the earth.'

The end of the blessed fortnight came, and Stephen and Emma returned to work. Even now, Mr Blunt and Miss Grace were besieged by anxious American clients, European tours were cancelled, and one or two elderly people wept.

Stephen was worried about the financial future of England, but Emma and Agnes could not bring themselves to be inter-ested. Their lives centred around him and Paul. In the mean-time, business at the car salesroom was dropping off and commissions were far less frequent. He pointed this out to Emma, who only said, 'It will pick up again, won't it?'

They saw more of the Hoods. Mr Hood had largely recovered from his fright but had had, he said, to draw in his horns and must look for a smaller house. He no longer complained so vigorously about Noel's paper-round. At the weekends they would often all come to Emma's flat to see the baby. Noel was particularly enthralled. 'You must get to know your uncle, old man,' he said, and he climbed into the play-pen to encourage Paul with his walking. Noel was just fourteen, and showed signs of cleverness.

'I hope he'll go to a university, unlike me,' Stephen said, 'but God knows how we're going to afford it, even on a grant.'

'If that time comes,' said Emma firmly – she was very fond of Noel – 'we shall have to help. I don't know how, but we will.'

'Give me my grandson to hold,' said Mrs Hood, with her broad, Sylvia-like smile. 'I see little enough of him.'

But Paul, perversely, was not to be distracted from his pen and cried until he was put back there.

'That's no way to receive your grannie,' said Mrs Hood, disconcerted.

'It's Noel who has seduced him,' Emma explained. 'If he gets out now, Paul should be more amenable.'

Noel obediently scrambled over the top of the pen, but still Paul would not go to his grandmother. He was playing with bricks, an abstracted look upon his face.

'He'll be all right in a few minutes,' Emma said, for the first time ashamed of her son.

They went to the Hoods again for Christmas, but this time taking the turkey and two bottles of wine. Paul went in his carry-cot. He was getting rather big for it and was happier sitting on Emma's knee, but the cot would be useful for his afternoon sleep. Sylvia had decorated a tree for him with baubles, tinsel and coloured lights, and Noel carried him round and round it. He reacted with joy and tried to clutch at the ornaments as he passed. 'We ought to have had a little tree for him at home,' Agnes said. 'We will, next year.'

They had their Christmas dinner late, at 3 p.m., and Paul did not like the crackers, though he ate a spoonful of finely minced turkey. Emma, somewhat emboldened by wine, drank a toast to her in-laws. 'The kindest I could have,' she said. They toasted her and the baby in return. All in all, it was a harmonious festivity.

The New Year came without remark. Paul had his first birthday and Agnes made a cake with a single candle on it, which Stephen had to blow out for him. Life continued to be placid for the four of them. In 1931 England went off the gold standard and Emma's agency was once more in ferment. Mr Blunt sent off a circular letter to all customers. Miss Grace left the firm at last, and Emma was promoted but with only ten shillings a week more money.

Agnes had a new client, a man called John Winter, whom she interviewed in the sitting-room, trying to ignore the play-pen. He was a man of about fifty, tall and personable, an architect, and he had a lot of work for her which was too much for his secretary. He called several times and, during the course of this, learned much about her, her widowhood, how she kept house for her daughter and son-in-law.

'I wonder if I might take you out to dinner one night,' he said, 'if you could be spared?'

She was bewildered by his obvious admiration. 'I don't really know – I don't go out much.'

'Just a quiet dinner. It would hardly be like going out. Please come.'

'I'll have to let you know.'

She consulted Emma. 'I feel such a fool, at my age. I don't know what to say.'

'He's no older than you are. Say yes; it will do you good. Is he married, by any chance?'

'He was once, but he's divorced. His wife ran away with his best friend – I gather it was a tragedy at the time, but he's got over it.'

'Well, it's good for you to have a flame. It would be good for you to marry again.'

'Don't be silly. What would you do without me? But it will never come to that.'

She went to the dinner, giving away her desire to do so by buying a new dress for the occasion in a bright shade of pink, which suited her. He asked her out again a fortnight later, but this time she refused. She had too much work piling up. Nevertheless, he continued to persist. 'At my age,' she kept repeating to Emma and Stephen, who pooh-poohed her.

Winter was obviously well-to-do. On their first outing he had taken her to the Monseigneur, in Jermyn Street, and on their second to Quaglino's, where they had danced. Agnes was unused to such luxury, and she enjoyed it, while feeling guilty for every hour she spent away from Stephen and Emma. They, to make her feel more comfortable, allowed her to mind the baby for them twice a week. Winter asked to meet them, and they approved of him. They were not sure that he was serious about Agnes, but were prepared to countenance the outings. The weeks went by for them all very happily.

On a bright morning in November, Stephen received an American customer who was much taken by an Alfa-Romeo and wanted a test-drive. Scenting a commission, Stephen consulted the manager of his firm, made a test-inspection of the client's licence and credentials, and agreed to accompany him. The client drove, Stephen beside him in the front seat. Just as they reached Hyde Park Corner, the car went out of control and crashed into the side of a lorry. Driver and passenger were killed instantly.

Part Two

Chapter One

THE NEWS was in the midday papers, because Stephen was young, his wife so young and his son, too.

The doctor came and put Emma under sedation. She lay between weeping and sleeping. Agnes coped with Paul as best she might, though he, sensing that something was wrong, was upset and fractious, constantly asking for Mummy and Daddy.

Mrs Hood and Sylvia came, red-eyed, and Emma drowsily mourned with them. Sylvia went into the living-room in search of Agnes and found Paul crying in his play-pen.

'Is there anything I can do to help?' Sylvia asked. 'I could put announcements in *The Times* and the *Telegraph.*'

'Yes, do that, and then, if you could bring yourself to play with Paul a little. . . .'

'I shall have to ask Emma how she wants it worded.'

But Emma was able only to murmur, 'My adored husband.' She relapsed into sleep, and Mrs Hood came away.

Agnes, who was still in a state of shock, helped with the rest of the wording.

Suddenly, in a road accident, Stephen, aged 25, adored husband of Emma and father of Paul, beloved son of Henry and Hattie Hood, brother of Sylvia and Noel.

When this had been dispatched, Sylvia got into the play-pen and managed to comfort Paul. Her mother was taken by the police to identify the body. She returned trembling, and Agnes made tea.

When Mrs Hood and Sylvia had both gone, an unexpected caller came. It was Eric Flowers, older, but as dapper as ever, whom they had not seen for two years. 'I came to see what

I could do. Perhaps I could make the funeral arrangements.'

'There will have to be an inquest,' Agnes said, 'but then you can help. Thank you, Eric.'

'They met on my veranda.' For a moment he, too, was overcome, but managed to pull himself together.

'I have to feed Paul now and get him to bed. He's very upset. It is almost as if he knew.'

John Winter sent flowers and the offer of any help he could give. Agnes felt a sense of relief that he was there.

The next morning the letters began to arrive, among them a postcard in a familiar disguised hand.

SO HUBBY'S KICKED THE BUCKET HA HA IN THE MIDST OF LIFE WE ARE IN DEATH. BUT MUMMY IS LESS GIDDY NOW.

This Agnes tore into small pieces and flushed down the lavatory.

Emma got up and dressed. She said, in a tone strangely steely, that she would answer all the letters as they arrived, even though the writers insisted that no reply was called for. She took Paul over again and even managed to play with him a little.

It was a bitterly cold day, the last chrysanthemums rotting in the wind. She wrapped Paul very warmly and put him in his pram in the small front garden for his sleep. Agnes wanted to care for him again but was met with a refusal. 'No, Mamma, thank you. You've done quite enough.'

So her mother confined herself to shopping and cooking, but could not make Emma eat anything. She had a glass of Bovril in milk, but that was all. It was painful to watch her dumb stoicism. She could not cease from some sort of activity. She packed up Stephen's clothes and addressed them to the Red Cross. She wrote letter after letter of thanks. Some were old schoolfriends of her husband's, unknown to her, paying tribute to the gentleness of his character. They could not give her consolation.

Late that evening, when she was back in bed, John Winter came. He put his arms round Agnes and kissed her. She accepted the kiss. She thought of him as a 'tower of strength'.

'You'll be having a hard time in the future,' he said. 'Don't go wanting for money; just let me know.'

Agnes, in the black dress she had worn for Reggie and never put on since, thanked him warmly but said she expected they would manage. Anyway, they would try. When he left, he kissed her cheek again.

The coroner, as expected, brought in a verdict of accidental death. The lorry-driver, whose fault it had not been, escaped with some cuts and bruises. The funeral took place at St Mark's Church, and Stephen was buried in the cemetery near by. All through the service Emma did not cry; she felt that she would never cry again, as if all the tears had been drained from her. She, like Agnes, was wearing black; Stephen had expressed no wish about this one way or another, but she felt the urge to do so. Sylvia remained behind to look after Paul, who had not yet ceased calling for 'Daddy'.

In the weeks that followed Emma was plagued by bodily needs. She would lie awake in the dark, remembering how close Stephen had been, how admirably they had fitted each other. Her whole being ached and beseeched, but there was no one to listen. She wondered how she was to get through life without him. She had left the agency and was uncertain what to do next. By the wills exchanged just after her marriage, she received the whole of his savings, which amounted to just over five hundred pounds. Yes, she would have to work again, but not yet, not yet. Agnes worked furiously at her typing, taking on rather more than she could manage. Winter supplied her with much of it, and she had just received the manuscript of a novel out of the blue. Day after day she and Emma ate almost in silence. 'You should get out somewhere,' Sylvia told them, 'even if it's only to the pictures. I'll sit with Paul.' So one night they went, but Emma felt no comfort. She kept remembering how often Stephen had sat there with her, and, for the first time since the day of his death she did cry a little in the darkness.

Not a success? Perhaps it was, because from that evening her love for Paul returned and she could hardly bear to let him out of her sight. Before bedtime, when he was on his pot, she sang to him from her repertoire of songs, which delayed things considerably as he loved them so much. She sang 'Speed, Bonny Boat,' and 'When Daffodils Begin to Peer', to a tune of her own devising. This he liked best of all, and would cry: 'Sing "Dabodoo", Mummy.' He was dry now by day and by night. In the mornings she would play with him in his pen and encourage his walking. He could now walk half-way across the room into her arms. Sometimes he said, 'Where's Daddy?' and she could only answer, 'He's gone away for a while.' 'Daddy come back?' 'Not yet, darling.'

As for Agnes, she had been unable to resist the flying thought: At last I have my daughter to myself. She tried to repress it, knowing it was wrong, but could not.

Stephen's firm had been good to them, paying Emma what would have been his six months' wages and taking his car off her hands. She bought Paul a push-chair for his expeditions to Battersea Park. He now wore a sailor-suit, of which he was very proud. When he sat on her knee he clung to her as if he would never let her go; he no longer had tantrums or crying fits but became equable again. His resemblance to Stephen increased; he had his smile, which would cause Emma's heart to move. Every night about seven o'clock she found herself listening for the sound which never came, Stephen's key in the lock.

Mr Hood took to visiting them. He had recovered from his first grief at the death of his son, and was now prepared to see his small replica. He was tender with Emma. 'You're a good girl. You'll always be my girl.' He taught Paul to throw a pingpong ball, and was tireless in picking it up again.

Sylvia, who had a new job, came to them once a week, and Issie did the same. Issie was gentler now, and did not criticise Emma; it was as if she had suddenly grown very fond of her niece. She was at heart a kind woman, though her life had been a disappointment. She had lost Reggie to her sister. She, too, would have liked to be married and have children, but now she was over fifty and all hope had gone. Like Miss Plimsoll her bark had always been worse than her bite, though in Miss Plimsoll's case, Emma thought, there might not always be a distinction between the two.

Eric Flowers had faded away again into his own rather

mysterious river-life. Once he asked Emma down, but she did not go, dreading all memories.

John Winter had gone to America, and for two months they did not see him. In the spring he returned, bringing stockings for Emma, an evening bag for Agnes, and for Paul a clockwork bear that walked as fast as the baby did. He asked both Agnes and Emma to dine out with him and took them to a quiet restaurant in St James's. A month later he asked Emma out by herself, and Agnes, bewildered, could not suppress a start of jealousy. But, he explained, he needed to get to know Emma better. Emma herself was suspicious of his motives, but agreed to go.

During the meal he spoke of Paul, easily of Stephen. 'I know how you must miss him,' he said, 'and I think you've been very brave.'

Not until the coffee was on the table did he say, 'I hope some day to marry your mother, though I haven't asked her yet. Would you mind?'

Emma was jolted. The thought flitted: But what should I do without her? She answered, 'I don't know.'

'You must always have realised that it was a possibility? She's an attractive woman. And I should take care of you and Paul. You needn't have that to worry about. Tell me, have you any objections to myself as me?'

She said no, but that the idea had been a shock to her.

'We're both much about the same age. I think it should work out.'

'What does Mother think?'

'I don't know. I haven't asked her. I wanted to talk to you first. I would set you up in a larger flat, where you could have a nanny for Paul.'

'I don't need a larger one, and I can take care of Paul myself. Please don't let's talk about it any more, just now.'

'As you please. But I wanted you to know how I felt. I can trust you to say nothing of this to Agnes. I am a lonely man and I need her. You need not be a lonely girl; I should see to that.' He spoke to her then about new films, new books, new plays, until it was time for them to go. He took her by taxi to her door but would not come in. 'Forgive me if I've disturbed you, Emma. Perhaps I shouldn't have said anything. But I didn't want you to be taken by surprise.'

Of course Agnes was eager to know about the evening. Where had he taken her? What did he want to say? Nothing much, Emma replied. 'We talked about Stephen and Paul. He said he would help us if we were in difficulties, but I told him we were all right at the moment.'

'Do you like him?'

'Yes. But he isn't easy to know.' Though Emma thought she knew him.

She speculated in bed that night. She had no idea how much her mother would be prepared for a proposal. She would probably say that she could not leave Emma, and Emma rather hoped she would. Agnes, by this time, had really become indispensable, and Emma believed that Winter would not let them live with him. She and Paul would be alone, and if she went back to work, which she felt she must do soon, she could not leave him alone all day. She was rather won over by the offer of a nanny, provided Paul did not come to love the woman more than herself. But all that was in the clouds, since she did not believe her mother would accept him when he asked her. A marriage would solve all their financial problems, but Emma would be left desolate. She remembered with compunction the way she and Stephen had danced round the sitting-room after sending Agnes off to Brighton. It would be like a revenge on them both. She spent an uneasy night.

Yet she was determined not to be selfish. It was hard to behave towards her as before, when Emma had not had possession of the secret. Agnes seemed as open as ever after her fortnightly dinners with Winter, and Emma wondered whether he had given the whole idea up. It was not until the summer that she realised he had not.

It was a hot summer's night. Agnes came home in a state of excitement. She was wearing her pink dress and she looked young and pretty. She said to Emma at once, 'I don't know what you think, but John has asked me to marry him!'

'I suspected something of the sort. What did you say?'

'That I would have to think things over. There were you and Paul to consider. He was so kind; he said he would never

88

let any of us want. Oh dear, it all seems so absurd at my age.'

'Mother,' Emma said firmly, 'if you do want to marry him you are not to let me and Paul stand in your way. On no account. Do you love John?'

'I don't know. I'm very fond of him.'

'I could be, too, if I had the chance. Darling' – this was an unaccustomed endearment – 'I suppose you wouldn't be going far away.'

'He's buying a house in Sloane Avenue. That's less than half a mile. But how would you cope? He's talking of getting you a nanny.'

'If you accepted him, I should accept the nanny.' She kissed Agnes on the cheek. 'Your talk went a long way.'

'Well, he would explore every possibility until I was quite bewildered. I wanted to ask if you and Paul could come and live with us, but I didn't dare.'

'Paul and I would never dream of it – and I mean that. You must make your own life. You've had little enough of it.'

'John is quite rich. You know that?'

'And do you let that weigh with you?' Emma felt like the mother, Agnes the child.

'I don't know. I expect it does a little,' Agnes answered honestly. 'But I am fond of him.'

'Enough to accept him?'

'Oh, don't rush me. I must have time to think. But I wanted you to know.'

'No more typing. Think of that!'

'I believe you want to get rid of me.' Agnes, for the first time, sounded a little tearful.

'One thing I insist on. If you do go, you'll take that damned parrot with you. She tried to bite me again when I fed her tonight. And, if John won't take Polly, it's all off.' She was trying to make her mother smile.

'Where would you go?'

'I should stay here. A nanny could have your room.'

'I have been a good mother to you?' Agnes sounded forlorn.

'You know you have. Too good.' In the emotion of the moment, Emma forgot her inhibitions about praise. 'Well, are you going to accept him?'

'It's early days yet.'

'I tell you what. We've some sherry left. We shall drink, at any rate, to your proposal.'

Chapter Two

AGNES agreed to marry John, and notices were put in *The Times* and the *Telegraph*. These brought her another postcard.

GETTING MARRIED AT YOUR AGE YOU OLD HAG. HA HA YOU MAKE ME LAUGH FIT TO SPLIT I EXPECT IT'S FOR MONEY THERE COULDN'T BE ANOTHER REASON.

This card, also, Agnes destroyed, but she was very upset. She hated the unseen presence.

The Hoods were told, and all expressed approval. She had their goodwill. Issie was less spontaneous. 'Well, I suppose you know your own mind, but it will make an upheaval.'

'I shall be able to take care of you a little, too.'

'Don't think of me. I'm getting along very nicely.'

'You must meet John soon. I'm sure you'll like him.'

'Yes, soon,' Issie replied, in a tone that meant she was in no hurry.

Sylvia talked things over with Emma; they were very close these days. 'Are you quite sure you won't mind, sweetie? You and your mother have been together so long.'

'I think it will be all for the best. I've insisted on her taking the parrot.'

Sylvia giggled. Then she said, 'Will you stay here?'

'Yes. It suits me. And, if I get the promised nanny, I shall take another job. I refuse to be entirely dependent upon John. Even if it's only a part-time job it will be something.'

'It's all such a surprise, isn't it? I wonder what Steve would have thought.' Sylvia could speak his name easily these days.

'I think he'd have been pleased.'

Winter had arranged to make Emma a generous allowance, which would cover the cost of the nanny. She tried to accept this without grudgingness. She was proud and hated to be under an obligation.

The three of them went together to see the house. It was a fine one, of only two storeys, with a white portico and Crittal-framed windows. There was a small garden at the back. 'You must think of it as your house, too,' he said to Emma awkwardly, as if she were a child, and she contrived a smile. Then Agnes became busy with curtains and carpetings, and took Emma and Paul together to choose them. Emma remembered the cheap and pretty curtains Agnes had made for their old house and she felt a pang. Even now her mother was not used to spending money, and tried to scrimp and save, but Emma would not let her. 'You can have the best. You buy it.' They chose velvet curtains of floor length and fitted carpets. Leaving Paul in the daily woman's care, Emma went to help her choose a dress for her wedding. 'Something very quiet,' Agnes said. 'I don't want to look dressed up.'

They were married in July, at Chelsea Registry Office. Issie was there, and the Hoods, and Eric Flowers. Afterwards they went to a restaurant for lunch. Agnes was much flushed and ill at ease; Winter seemed transported with happiness. They were going for a brief honeymoon in the Lake District; Winter had wanted to go to France, but Agnes did not want to leave England. She was tearful when it came to saying good-bye to Emma. 'I shall miss you terribly, darling.'

'Don't. You go and have a good time. All's well with Paul and me.'

So Emma went back to the flat alone, and next day the nanny came. She was a small, elderly woman with a lifetime's experience. Her name was Harcourt. When Emma had interviewed her she had asked, 'Do you want me to take sole charge?'

'Well, no, not sole.' She was put out by the question. 'I should want to share Paul with you.'

'Good. If you hadn't wanted that, I wouldn't have come. A child of that age needs his mother. Some of my ladies only saw their children at tea-time.' Obviously Nanny disapproved.

'This will be my last baby,' she continued. 'I'm getting on in years.'

When she was introduced to Paul, she took him on her knee and he beamed as if he had known her all his life. She was much touched, and kissed the top of his head.

She settled down well into the flat, though it was plain that she had known better days. 'I used to have an under-nurse-maid,' she told Emma, 'but that was long ago. And of course there was the cook.'

'I'm the cook,' Emma said, 'and we shall have our meals together.'

Nanny's presence made it easier for her not to listen for the sound of the latchkey and the clicking of the typewriter through the wall. The parrot had been duly installed in her new home, and had begun badly by trying to bite Winter. Emma was glad to see the back of her.

Nanny, who had a light job with Paul, made herself useful in other ways, knitting for him, mending Emma's under-clothes and sometimes helping with the washing-up. Emma was delighted with her, and very soon became fond of her. Nanny Harcourt was both philosophical and pragmatic. She took in her little short stride the disappearance of the old days, of her 'ladies', under-nursemaids and cooks, and devoted herself to the young widow and child. In the evenings she liked to sit knitting or sewing in her own room, listening to the wireless. She helped with the shopping, taking Paul in his push-chair with her, and after his afternoon sleep took him for an hour in the park. He speedily took to her. She bought him an old-fashioned ABC book – 'A was An Archer who shot at a frog' – and he began to learn his letters. Agnes, who called every other day, was chagrined to find him reluctant to leave Nanny's lap and come to her. 'You see,' she said to Emma, 'he's forgotten already.'

Nanny provided what seemed endless cups of tea, which Emma was compelled to drink. At nine o'clock at night she was offered tea or Ovaltine as a nightcap and accepted the former. She only clashed with Nanny on the question of putting lights on in the bedroom and refusing to tiptoe. He had not been brought up to it, she explained, and he never wakes. 'I think it disturbs him all the same,' said Nanny. 'I always had quiet in my nurseries.' So they managed to effect a kind of compromise, Emma tiptoeing but putting on the light to undress by.

In the autumn she got a part-time job, serving in the afternoons at a small dress-shop in the King's Road where she tried brightly to sell garments she considered very ugly. It brought her in a little money but not much, and Winter demurred at it.

'My dear child, you don't need to go there. You know you needn't.'

'But I like to do it,' she said. 'It gives Nanny more to do.'

'I believe you like Nanny better than me,' Agnes said jealously one day, 'and I'm sure Paul does. I knew it would be like that when I left you.'

'Don't be silly, Mummy,' said Emma.

She felt that she hardly knew her mother these days. Agnes, at Winter's instigation, was getting to be smart. There seemed no end to her new clothes. She had a housekeeper and two servants, but she still loved to cook, and Winter let her, though with reluctance. Sometimes she would ask Emma and her old friends to come in for the evening and prepare the floor for dancing, but somehow it was not as it had been. Perhaps they missed the bread pudding, which was not something she could explain to her husband.

'Why did you never marry?' Emma asked Nanny Harcourt curiously one evening when they were at supper.

Nanny smiled her small lemony smile. 'That's my secret. Perhaps I was asked, perhaps I wasn't. But I always loved babies and this is my way of having them.'

'Lucky babies,' said Emma. 'I bet you were asked, though.'

Nanny gave her a glance of gratification. 'If I ever was, it's a long time ago.'

She had expressed admiration at Stephen's photograph. 'He looks a thoroughly nice young man.'

'Oh, he was.'

Confidence established itself. Emma asked, and was told, all about the 'ladies'. All were popular, it seemed, except for the ones who had not sent Christmas cards. 'One does like to keep in touch.' Three of the ladies had been titled and all of them rich. Several of her babies had grown up, married and had children of their own. By which Emma gathered that Nanny was a good deal older than she had thought.

Almost a year after Stephen's death a girl at Emma's dress-shop asked her one night to a small local club called Le Bistro. After much thought, she accepted; she had been out very little by herself since Nanny came. The place was in a cellar. There was a bar, a few tables and chairs and a small dance-floor. It was lit by candles in Chianti bottles. Emma had never been to a night-club before but soon found that there was nothing to be afraid of. She and Helen drank beer, and partners came to them. One was a dark young man of middle height who took an immediate fancy to Emma. 'My name's Denzil,' he said as they danced. 'What's yours?' She told him, and he asked whether she often came there. No, she said, it was the first time. 'I hope you'll come again often. Please do.' He joined her at her table, while Helen and another man went on dancing. 'I see you're married, though,' he said looking down at her hand. 'I was. My husband died.' 'I'm sorry.' Though he did not look as if he were. When the evening came to an end, he asked if he might see her home. It was nearly midnight. 'If you like,' she said.

'Do you live alone?'

'With my small son and his nanny.'

On their way back, he told her he was a student of physics at Imperial College. He was twenty-two years of age; the same as herself.

When they reached her door he said, 'May I come in? Just for a cup of coffee? I won't stay long.'

She hesitated.

'Please.'

So she let him in and they walked very quietly up the stairs. Nanny was in bed but not asleep. 'Is that you, M'm?'

'Yes. I've brought a friend back. How's Paul?'

'Sleeping like an angel. Didn't half enjoy his supper.'

'Go back to sleep now. It's late. Good-night.'

It seemed very bright in the sitting-room after the candle-lit club and the dark streets. He sat beside her on the divan. 'Do you know you're beautiful, Emma?'

She answered nervously, 'I seldom get called that.'

'But you are. I couldn't help saying it.'

'I must go and make the coffee.'

'No, don't. I don't really want it. Stay here with me.'

He kissed her and she responded. Her heart was beating heavily and the loneliness of the year worked upon her. He fondled her breasts gently, and she knew an uprush of desire. She felt excited and guilty.

'Don't.'

'I want you, Emma.'

'And don't say that. We hardly know each other.'

But she wanted him, too – or, rather, wanted his body. She did not care if she never saw him again. He unfastened her blouse and continued to caress her.

She tried to resist. 'I haven't let a man do that since – since – I'm not like that. You must go home.'

'Let me make love to you, Emma.'

She let him undress her, terrified all the time that Nanny would wake.

'You're beautiful,' he said again.

In this lovely nightmare they stared at each other. They lay down side by side. He was experienced, rousing her still further by play, until at last he took her. Almost at once she had an orgasm and he was quick to follow. 'Beautiful,' he said. Drained and exhausted, she rose and started to dress again. He was slower. 'Thanks,' he said. 'You're a wonderful girl. When am I going to see you again?'

'Never. It was only this once. You must understand that. I feel guilty enough as it is.'

'Why should you? You were lonely.'

'Very lonely. That's why it was. But never again.'

'Don't say that. I'm crazy about you.'

'I do say it. I'm not one of those girls who sleep with anybody.'

'I can tell you're not. I wouldn't take advantage.'

'You really must go home now. And I do thank you; it's been over a year. But it must never happen again.'

'If I promise?'

'No. We mustn't meet again.'

'You'll be coming to Le Bistro?'

'No.' Already she felt like a whore. Would the anonymous letter-writer find out and confirm it? When at last he had gone, refusing to accept her ban, she undressed again and got into bed.

She did not say her prayers that night, feeling unworthy to say them. She did not kiss Paul in his sleep. She felt unworthy of that, too. Her early religious training, never far dormant, preyed on her. She had broken a Commandment. She had not been attracted by him except physically, and that made it all the worse. She was conscious of sin. Yet she slept at once, and dreamed of herself in childhood, sitting with her mother at St Mark's, under Mr Mossop.

When she had fed Paul and made breakfast for herself and Nanny, next morning, Nanny commented on her appearance. 'You look peaky, M'm. It must have been that late night.'

'Perhaps. I'm rather tired.'

Winter went to his club two nights a week, and Agnes either went to see Emma, or asked Emma to visit her. The morrow was one of those nights, and Agnes came to the flat. She, also, noticed Emma's pallor. 'Why, what have you been doing to yourself?' she said.

And Emma confessed to her, seeking absolution.

As expected, Agnes was horrified. 'Whatever made you do that?' she said.

Emma poured out how great her physical longing had been. Agnes could not understand it at all, and Emma wondered what her sexual life with Winter, if any, was like. She told her uncomprehending mother about her sense of sin, and of betrayal. She had betrayed Stephen. 'But some nights I can't sleep because of wanting him.'

'So you picked up a boy at a club?' said Agnes. 'I don't know how you could. But I'm glad you've told me. As a child, you used to tell me everything.' This was her delusion.

'Yes, or, rather, he picked me up.'

'It all sounds so vulgar,' Agnes said.

'It wasn't like that at all. You don't know at all how I've suffered without Stephen.'

'You didn't think of Paul?'

Emma, stung, replied that she didn't know what he had to do with it. 'I should never have told you.'

97

'It's better that you should have. Darling' – this indicated that her mother was softening – 'don't think of it too much. I'm sure the Lord would forgive you. But this is what came of my going away. Do you think I don't feel guilt, too?'

'There's no reason why you should,' said Emma, forlorn.

Chapter Three

SHE never confided in intimacy to her mother again. She fancied she had told Winter all about her. He was as kind to her as ever, but it seemed to her that he had a new air of appraisal and she was ill at ease with him. Did they tell each other everything? Some married couples did. She and Stephen had. But she had not suspected that Agnes would betray her. Emma withdrew more and more into her shell.

She refused to revisit Le Bistro, despite the urgings of her friend in the dress-shop. 'But why won't you? I thought you'd got off properly the other night. Didn't you fancy him?' Not very much, Emma had said. She gave the excuse that she didn't like to be so long away from the baby. Denzil wrote to her once, addressing the envelope to 'Mrs Hood' – so he must have got her name from the slip of cardboard underneath the bell-push. She did not reply, and he ceased to trouble her, though for some little time she jumped when the telephone rang. She guessed that he had found somebody else. It would not be difficult for him. She tried to put the memory of that evening out of her mind.

She went out less and less, and Nanny Harcourt remarked this. 'You never seem to go to the pictures or anything, M'm. You know Paul's safe with me.'

'I know he is, Nanny. It's just that I don't care to go about much.' Winter took Agnes on a trip to America shortly after the New Year. He asked Emma to come, too. She thanked him gratefully, but refused. She did not, she said, like to be too long away from her son.

'Oh, nonsense,' Agnes said, 'you've got Nanny. You'd enjoy being on a ship, wouldn't you? You could buy some new dresses for it.' But Emma was obdurate. She thought

Winter liked her the less for this, but could not be certain; he had always been something of an enigma to her.

While they were away she did a little entertaining, taking pleasure in the cooking, and refused to let Nanny withdraw to her room when guests came. One night she asked Sylvia and Noel (now sixteen) and Ann and her husband. On another, her parents-in-law and Dicky and his new wife. Both occasions were successful; even the soufflé, into which she had put such care, did not sink. Mrs Hood complimented her. 'You've become a fine little cook. I'm quite outclassed.'

'I'm sure you're not. But Grannie taught me all I knew, even when she was blind. She would sit by me and give me directions. Sometimes she'd try and catch me out. "You've given the mince an hour, I suppose?" (Triumphantly) "Well, you shouldn't. Fifteen is quite enough." I used to feel such a fool.'

She bought herself new clothes. He had said that she was beautiful.

Gradually she grew more in conceit with herself. She thought of Denzil only when her desires almost overcame her.

One night when they were alone, she confessed to Ann what had happened. She could not confess to Sylvia. The act of confession brought tears to her eyes. 'I felt like a whore.'

'Don't be so silly, darling. I can imagine what it's like to be without Stephen. And he wouldn't have blamed you.'

'I wonder. I blame myself.'

'Listen, I've had a man or two.'

'You have?' Emma was amazed. 'But, then, it can't have been on a first meeting.'

'Pretty near it, love. And I haven't suffered pangs of remorse. They're simply not for me. And I haven't felt a need to confess. I'm only telling you because I want you to know that you're not the only girl with her slip showing. You took precautions, I hope?'

'Not even that. It was all too sudden. But nothing has happened.'

'Lucky you. It might have done. Then you'd really have something to cry about. Just try to remember what nice times we all had together in the twenties. Dicky with his ukulele – did you know that his wife was pretty well-off?'

'And the bread pudding.' Emma tried to smile.

'And Aunt Issie bringing in the clock! Those were the days.'

Emma said, when Ann was leaving, 'You've done me so much good. I'm sorry to have wept all over you.'

'That's what friends are for. I'll weep all over you whenever I feel the need, which isn't often.'

Emma thought of Ann when she had gone, how she took things in her stride, and she envied her. But she was grateful and felt a little released from her sense of sin. She took to going to Chelsea Old Church again on Sunday mornings, which was heartily approved by Nanny.

'You could go in the evenings,' she said.

'Yes, I suppose I could. I like to hear the hymns and a good sermon, though we're Congregationalist in my family. Always have been. But I don't much mind where I go, provided it's not to the Catholics of course.'

So every Sunday morning Emma went to church, and Nanny every Sunday evening. This appeased them both, and Nanny, when she returned, could always give an account of the service. '"The Day Thou Gavest,"' she said. 'I always liked that.'

Emma derived, from her new churchgoing, both comfort and fear. The Lord forgave to seventy times seven. Emma did not believe in Hell really, but was frightened by the thought of the everlasting bonfire. She remembered the bonfire on Guy Fawkes Night in their old garden, and how her father had joyously stamped it out. She remembered Floss White fainting in the *Macbeth* class, and Miss Sumnour's brief panic. Her early youth came back to her in a rush of reminiscence. I was so happy then. Am I ever really happy now? Sometimes, when I play with Paul or take him out.

She gave up selling ugly, badly sewn dresses, and got another part-time job in an antique dealer's. This did not pay much, but it taught her a good deal. She developed an eye for good furniture, and when she visited Agnes again was able to tell how wisely Winter had bought.

'The only thing I miss is having a cat or a dog, but John says they spoil everything with their claws.' She told Emma about the American trip. 'Doesn't it make your mouth water? But you must come next time. We should both like you to.'

'That's very kind of you and John,' Emma answered. 'But I should have to think about it.'

That month Nanny Harcourt went home to Cambridge for a week to be with her sister. Agnes called every day to do what she could for Emma.

She was charmed by Paul's progress. He was reading now, simple words taught him by Emma, 'pig', 'cow', 'hen', 'cat'. He could spell out 'Mummy' and 'Daddy' and his own name in his alphabet bricks. He did not ask about Stephen now; it was as if he had accepted the fact of death or, at least, of a situation in which there was to be no return. He was walking well now, and often insisted on getting out of his push-chair when Emma or Agnes took him to the shops. He retained his loathing of carrots and his liking for the evening songs. Agnes sometimes sang Gilbert and Sullivan to him, too, and he liked that, though he preferred Emma's singing.

Noel was in his last year of the grammar school, and he hoped to go up to Oxford on a scholarship. The grant wouldn't be adequate, Sylvia said, but she would work herself to the bone to keep him there. He was still greatly attracted by his nephew, and Emma taught Paul to spell out 'Uncle Noel' in bricks.

Paul loved him. 'I wish Uncle Noel would come and live with us,' he said, and Emma was realising that he treated this boy as a surrogate parent. She told this to Agnes, who said rather nervously, 'Have you ever thought of marrying again?'

Emma said, 'I don't see the men beating a path to my door.'

'It would be so good for Paul. And if men don't beat a path to your door it's because you don't go out anywhere. That's one of the reasons I want you to come to America. Anything may happen on shipboard.'

'Not to me. And honestly, Mamma, I don't want to go. I'm happy enough as I am.'

'But you must be so lonely.'

'Not with you and Nanny and Paul.'

Agnes took her hand for a moment, then dropped it. They were sitting at supper, Paul in bed and the house quiet.

'When I think of what you told me—'

'Don't, Mamma. I'm sorry I did.'

'But it made me realise how much you miss Stephen.'

'There's bread pudding for sweet. It can't be as nice as yours was, but there's lots of peel in it.'

'So I'm snubbed.'

'No, you aren't. Only I don't want to talk about things.'

Agnes ate the pudding almost in silence and praised it.

She said, 'John's giving me a fur coat.'

'Lucky you. He is kind, isn't he? What will it be – mink?'

'I don't think we're all that rich. I shall have to look around. Will you help me, when Nanny comes back?'

'I'd love to. It would be exciting.'

'We'll spend the whole morning on it and then have lunch out. We might buy you something, too.' The idea of an outing with her daughter much pleased Agnes; she had felt that they were growing apart. So they had their expedition. Agnes bought a sealskin coat and persuaded Emma to accept a dress. 'I like to think of you looking smart, darling.'

'I like to look smart, too. Thank you very much, Mamma.'

Sylvia invited Emma to an evening party.

She issued her invitation. Emma said, 'Shall I bring Mummy?' But Sylvia, to her surprise, gave a positive No. 'You're with your mamma too much. We never see you without her, and this is a party for young people. You don't mind me saying so? Everybody says it.'

'I don't mind,' Emma said slowly, 'but it seems so strange these days.'

'I'm sorry if it does. But there it is.'

And Emma accepted.

She had not resented what Sylvia had said, but she was troubled by it. Had all her friends felt that her mother was too omnipresent? Yet they had seemed to welcome her.

She wore the new dress. Mr and Mrs Hood were out, so Sylvia had the house to herself. It remained unsold, and now none of them was prepared to move.

'Emma, I want you to meet Alan Priest. Alan, my sister-in-law. She's a sweetie.'

He was a tall man, nearer forty than thirty. He had a plain, roughly structured face with fine light eyes. 'Come and sit by me,' he said. 'I'll bring you some more wine.'

'Thank you, but I think I've had enough.'

'Well, I haven't, so do join me.' As he crossed the room she saw that he had an athlete's figure, loose-limbed with slightly sloping shoulders. 'There you are,' he said, when he came back. 'Get this down you and you'll be in the party spirit.' He was a little unsteady on his feet. He seemed to know all about Emma and told her something of himself. He was in a tea-merchant's in the City. 'So you can see why I'm not drinking tea now. It would be a busman's holiday.' He was thirty-eight years old and unmarried. 'And you've got a son,' he added.

Noel, who had come to sit on the sofa with them, said, 'He's a marvellous kid, my nephew.'

'You're young to be an uncle,' said Alan.

'That makes it all the more fun.'

'I won't ask you to dance,' Alan said. 'I'd bring you down on the floor.'

Sylvia, the carpet rolled up, was doing a modified Charleston with a young man.

'I can't do those fancy steps, Emma — your name is Emma?'

'It is, worse luck,' she replied.

'What would you have liked to be called?'

'Oh, I don't know, really. Joan or Mary, perhaps.'

'I shall call you Emma, because it makes me think of Jane Austen. Do you like her?'

'Only *Pride and Prejudice*. That was her only marriage that would have turned out well.'

When everyone was saying good-bye to Sylvia he said, 'I've got my car. I'll run you home.'

'That would be kind.'

She felt at ease with him, but did not really know why. He lived with an elderly aunt, he told her, in a house near Richmond Park. 'She's getting old,' he said, 'but she's still active. She runs things for me. My parents are dead. It's an odd sort of life, but it suits me well enough. I play golf or tennis at the week-ends.'

'I'm afraid I don't play anything,' she said, 'because I hate running about, but I think I might like golf.'

'No running there. I must teach you.'

They had come to her door. As he let her out of the car he said, 'Good-night. I shall see you soon.'

Back in the flat, she was bewildered. Yes, it did seem an odd life for a man of his age. She wondered whether he might be homosexual, but soon dismissed the thought. He had seemed too much attracted by her, though he had not kissed her. She wondered about Sylvia's motive in bringing them together. Does *she* think I ought to get married again? And what about Stephen? Her thoughts flew ahead of her. Richmond Park would be pleasant for Paul, though she did not like the idea of living with an old woman. But this is absurd! I've only met him the once.

She was sufficiently attracted to hope that he would soon get in touch with her, but it was nearly a week before he telephoned. Would she care to come for a drive on Sunday afternoon? They could go to tea at the Maids of Honour, on Richmond Hill, and then on for a drink at the golf club.

'I thought you didn't like tea,' she teased him.

'I don't much; but I like those splendid little cakes. Will you come? I promise you'll be home by seven.'

'I'd like to. What time will you pick me up?'

So it was arranged.

Chapter Four

SUNDAY was a fine mild March day, small white clouds like puffs from gunshot scattered over the bright sky. The daffodils and almond blossom were out in the London squares.

Alan was early, coming just before Emma had finished dressing. She asked him in, and introduced him to Paul, who was in his pen.

'This is Mr Priest.'

'Mister Beasht!' Paul cried joyously.

'That's not right, old man. Mr Prr–eest. Try to say that.'

'Beasht,' Paul repeated, filled with merriment.

'I think you'd better call me Alan. It's easier. Can he come out of there?' Alan asked Emma.

'If you like to stop him swarming all over the place. I shan't be five minutes.'

When she came back he had Paul on his knee, still crying, 'Mr Beasht!'

'I'm ready now,' she said, crying out, 'Nanny, I'm off. I'll be back by half past seven.' She gave her trip an extra half-hour, knowing what it would be like.

She was wearing the dress Agnes had given her, even though she feared he might think she had only the one dress to wear. But it was her smartest.

'What do you think of that chap Hitler?' Alan asked as they drove away.

'I haven't thought of him much.'

'Don't you read the papers? You know, my girl, you mustn't be deaf and blind. He's going to be a menace.'

'I'll try to learn about politics, if you will instruct me.'

'But you don't know the ABC! However, it's too fine a day for that.'

They spent an hour or so in the park, where the deer were roving, and went on to the tea-shop on Richmond Hill, where they both consumed the speciality, 'maids of honour', for which the recipe was obscure. The shop was full, everyone's spirits uplifted by the sun. Emma and Alan dawdled over their tea. He asked her more about herself, but never seemed impertinent, and she answered him freely.

'What's it like, bringing the boy up all by yourself?'

'Not all by myself. There's Nanny. My stepfather pays for her and she's worth every farthing of it.'

'Shall we go to the pictures next week, and see *Queen Christina*? Do you like Garbo? I think she's the most beautiful woman I've ever seen.'

She said she did, and felt lowered by her inability to compete.

'I hope you'll come out with me often,' he said. 'I should like it.'

'We'd have to see how I'm fixed—'

'Nonsense. You've got Nanny.'

'But I don't like to take advantage. How long have you known Sylvia?'

'About three years. I like her very much.'

'So do I. I like them all.'

'They are good in-laws?'

'Very good. I couldn't wish for better.'

'You're young to be by yourself, with a growing child. He's a fine boy, by the way. I like him, though he will call me "Beasht" for the rest of my days.'

She looked at his by no means handsome profile. Only the brow and the eyes were fine. She was attracted to him, but hardly knew why. He had not flirted with her, he had not made her embarrassed. They went at last to the golf club. The club-house was warm and crowded. He sat her down at a table, brought a gin and tonic for her and a double whisky for himself. 'It's rather soon after tea,' she said.

'But if I'm to keep my promise and deliver you home sevenish, we must make a start now.'

'What's your handicap?' she asked. She knew that much about the game.

107

'Four. You must come round with me some time – that is, if you like walking. You might find it interesting.'

She said she was sure she should. He introduced her to the secretary of the club, a Captain something or other, and his wife. He got them to join Emma and himself. 'What are you having?'

He had finished his whisky, but Emma would not have another gin. 'You forget,' she said, 'I've parental duties to perform.'

'There won't be much to do with Nanny there,' he replied shrewdly. 'Paul will be in bed, or ought to be, if there's any discipline in your household.'

'Precious little. But, yes, he will be in bed, though I've got to get Nanny's supper and mine.'

'A nanny!' the captain's wife exclaimed. 'I could do with one for mine. Aren't you the lucky one?'

'I am, in that respect,' Emma answered. 'How many children have you got?'

They talked about the children for ten minutes, while the men refilled their glasses. The captain's wife put her hand over hers.

Twilight was coming on, and more people were coming in from the course. The lights were turned on. At a quarter to seven Alan looked at his watch and said, regretfully, 'Well–p?'

'Indeed, well–p,' she said. 'I really must be getting back.'

'One for the road?'

She declined, and thanked him.

'You play?' the captain asked.

'I'm afraid not.'

'Let Alan teach you, and then you can join us. It's a jolly club.'

'I can see that it is.'

'That's a lovely dress,' said the captain's wife. They talked clothes for a few minutes while Alan waited behind Emma's chair.

'We really will be late,' he said.

The traffic was heavy, and it was nearly eight before she got home. She thanked him for a lovely day.

'I have to thank you. Let's have more of them.'

When she was indoors, she thought she must pay more attention to the papers. She read them after a fashion, but without much thought. She had read about the rise of Hitler but knew little about him. She had been too wrapped up in Paul.

Now she wanted to please Alan, so much her senior. She admired him for the way in which he had made no advances to her, only suggesting that they meet often. Well, she would like that. She liked the ambience of his life, the park, the golf course, the club. It was all new to her and agreeable.

She was apologetic to Nanny. 'But I won't be long; there's only cold beef and I'll mash some potatoes. And there's some trifle left over from lunch.'

'You go and have a good time, M'm, and don't worry about me. I wish you went out more. By the by, it's time Paul had a bigger bed; the cot's getting too small for him. Could he have the other bed in your room?'

Of course, Emma replied, he would like that. She would like it, too.

'He hardly ever uses the pram now,' she said, 'nor the play-pen, though it's useful for keeping him out of mischief. We'd have to put a gate across the stairs. We might sell the cot and the pram and the pen.'

'We'll try him in the big bed tomorrow, shall we?' Nanny suggested. 'It'll make him feel ever such a big boy.'

Paul took to it with aplomb, only waking for a moment when Emma came to bed, to take advantage of a final good-night.

When Alan telephoned Emma next time to ask her to the pictures, she invited him to an early supper first. 'You'll have Nanny's company as well as mine, but she's very sweet. And we can go off afterwards.'

When he came he brought a bottle of gin and one of whisky, and they had a drink together. Even Nanny consented to a sip of sherry, which was the only liquor Emma kept in the house. He was charming to Nanny, and praised Emma's curry. 'I haven't had that in years. It's excellent.'

They went to see, not *Queen Christina*, but *The Testament of Dr Mabuse*, which scared Emma so badly that she was glad not to be going back to an empty house. 'Well, you were keen on it,' Alan said, 'and I don't expect you'll have nightmares. Sweet dreams.' He kissed her then, just a peck on the cheek.

'Well,' said Sylvia a week later, 'how are you getting on with our Alan, sweetie? He's taken a shine to you, I think, and I don't blame him.'

Emma said slowly, 'Sylvia, would you mind if I married again?'

Sylvia did not answer at once. Then she said, 'No, of course I shouldn't, darling. Stephen wouldn't have wanted you to be lonely for ever. Who have you got in mind?'

'Alan.'

'Has he asked you? He's never asked a girl before, so far as I know.'

'No. But I have a kind of instinct. If I'm wrong, you can call me a fool and laugh at me.'

'Are you in love with him?'

'Perhaps a little. Not more than that.'

Sylvia said, her good-humoured face a little troubled, 'But shouldn't it be more than that? Are you sure of what you're doing, sweetie?'

'I'm not sure of anything, even if I'll accept if he asks me. I think he'd be kind to Paul, and Paul needs a father.'

'It seems to me a rum sort of business. You do know that he's pretty well-heeled?'

'I guessed it.'

'Would that make a difference?'

'It couldn't help but make one, with Nanny and Paul to consider.'

'He's a nice chap, and we're fond of him. But do be careful what you're doing.'

'I haven't anything definite yet to be careful about.' Emma paused. 'There will never be anyone like Stephen. You may be sure of that.'

'That hardly sounds fair on Alan.'

'You sounded stern just then. I don't think you approve of me.'

'You know I do. We all do. But you've taken me by surprise. Is it too early to have a drink on it?'

Emma smiled. 'Much too early. But we will. Paul calls Alan "Mr Beasht", and can't be made to change his ways.'

'I always thought there was a bit of the devil in Paul, love though he is.'

Emma's instinct was not wrong. Shortly after that, Alan did ask her to marry him. 'I've never asked anybody else. But you're different. You and Paul would be safe with me. I love you very much.'

'I don't know what to say.'

'Take your time.' This time he kissed her properly, his tongue between her lips. She was moved, and aroused. 'I'll tell you all about my not-so-guilty past.'

There had been a girl, he said, some years ago, but it hadn't worked out. He had been content with a bachelor life, with his golf and tennis. He drank a bit, he confessed, but never too much. He had never been drunk, he said, in his life. He had been content with a bachelor existence. He had one brother, in Australia. 'When I get married, Aunt Daisy will go out to join him. She always said she would. I'll take you and Paul and Nanny to Richmond. It's fine and healthy there, and he can enjoy playing in the park. What do you say now?'

She said yes. She had not meant to say it so soon. He kissed her again. 'I know you don't love me as I love you, but you will in time.'

He made no attempt to take her to bed, and she was grateful to him. 'We'll wait,' he said, 'like proper married folk. I don't want anything to be spoiled.'

When he left her, her mind was in a turmoil. Did she really want this? Her body needed him, but for the rest she was not so sure.

After a turbulent night, she awoke to calm and to a resolution. She said to Paul, 'Would you like a new Daddy? I'm going to marry Alan.'

'Mr Beasht.'

'Hush, don't ever call him that again. You can call him "Papa", or "Alan", if you like.'

'Alan,' he said. 'Is Daddy coming back?'

'I'm afraid he never will, my darling.'

'Where's he gone?'

'To Jesus,' she said self-consciously.

'I don't want him to go to Jesus. I want him to come back here.'

'He never will, I'm afraid. But I'm going to take you to a lovely house near Richmond Park, where there are deer, and ferns as high as your head – higher.'

'Will Nanny come, too?'

'I hope so. I'm going to ask her.'

'I shall like to see the deer.'

'And you'll like Alan.'

'Like Alan,' he repeated.

Nanny, when the news was broken to her at breakfast, took it with sang-froid. 'Well, he seems a nice gentleman, M'm, and you oughtn't to be all on your own.'

'And you'll come, too? There will be plenty of room for you and Paul.'

'It's never mattered to me where I work. Richmond is nice. When's it to be, M'm?'

'It's not decided yet. Fairly soon.'

'Well, I'll take Paul out while it's still bright. Is there any shopping I can do for you?'

Emma gave her a list. 'You are kind, Nanny, and I do love you.'

Nanny looked gratified. But she said, 'I do hope Mr Priest is going to get fond of Paul. He won't be used to a child about the house.'

'He's fond of Paul already.'

Paul came toddling in. He had had his own breakfast and had been spelling out his own name with his bricks. 'Mummy's going to marry Daddy again,' he said confidently.

'No, but you're going to have a new daddy and live in a nice big house,' Emma said quickly.

'Where there will be deer.'

'Yes, love.'

'And Nanny will come, too.'

'Of course I will. Do you think I'd leave my own little man?'

'Nanny will never leave Paul. Never get married and go away.'

'I think I can promise you that,' said Nanny.

Chapter Five

EMMA broke the news to her mother, who was glad for her sake but surprised, and said she would soon bring Alan to see her and John.

'Come to dinner,' Agnes said, 'and we'll see what we make of him.'

'You'd better make something good of him,' Emma replied. Agnes had many questions to ask and was duly answered. Yes, he was well-off. He would care for Paul and Nanny. He was thirty-eight, not handsome, but with a nice smile. He was a tea merchant.

'But you've known him such a short while.'

'Only a few months. But it's enough.'

So Alan came to dine. Agnes and Winter received him warmly and congratulated him.

'I'm very lucky,' he said, 'and I haven't even bought Emma a ring yet. I was thinking of an emerald.'

She flushed. 'That would be lovely.'

He looked around the handsome room. 'What a fine house you have,' he said to Agnes.

'Do you like it? It's roomy.'

'Mine's roomy, too. I haven't even taken Emma to see it, up to now.'

He accepted a whisky and drank it straight off. Winter gave him another one, which he made to last him till dinner-time.

'I hope', he said to Agnes, over the meal, 'that when I show Emma my house you'll come, too. And you,' he added to Winter.

'I'd love to come,' she said, 'but I don't know whether John will be free.'

Alan asked Winter whether he played golf. No, was the answer, not these days. He had some arthritis in the shoulder.

'What do you do for recreation?'

'Well,' Winter answered smiling, 'it may sound absurd at our ages, but my wife and I often go dancing. She's a bit of an expert. I read a lot.'

'So do I,' said Alan, and to Emma this was unexpected. 'Mostly Kipling and Conrad. I've got a complete set of Kipling to date.'

'I fancy he's an acquired taste,' Winter said.

'He wasn't once,' said Emma. 'He was a universal one.'

'I read Trollope and Thackeray,' Winter put in. 'They're soothing. Or don't you suppose an architect needs to be soothed?' he said to Alan.

'I wouldn't know. But I've read *Barchester Towers*.'

'You need to read *The Last Chronicle of Barset* to see how good he really is.'

'I must try. I imagine Mrs Winter is a wonderful dancer. Anyway, Emma told me that she was.'

'I was taught all I know by one of Emma's young friends, many years ago.'

'Emma's quite good, too,' said Alan, 'but perhaps not in your class. Never mind, she's better at everything else.'

'When do you mean to marry?' asked Winter, nothing if not direct.

'In May. I wanted a registry office wedding, but Emma insists on church.'

'More satisfactory,' Winter said, 'and perhaps more lasting.'

'Ours will last anyway,' said Alan, giving Agnes his charming smile. 'I'm determined that it shall.'

The men stayed at table for half an hour, while Agnes and Emma went into the drawing-room.

'Well, do you like him?' Emma asked.

'What I've seen of him, yes,' said Agnes. 'Perhaps he's rather old for you. But, yes, I like him. He's got a nice face.'

'And wonderful eyes,' said Emma.

'Perhaps they are. How's he going to be with Paul?'

'A perfect papa, I hope. I have had to stop Paul calling him "Mr Beasht". It's irreverent.'

'It sounds as though Paul is being rather naughty. Can that be true?'

'It could be, yes. He's not an angel, bless him.'

'We all bless him. And Nanny? What does she think?'

'She's satisfied. By the way, John won't have to pay for her when we move. Alan will take her over.'

'As if he minded paying!'

'He's done a lot for me already. Don't think I haven't been grateful.'

'Well,' said Agnes, 'he deprived you of a mamma, so I suppose he thought he owed you something.' Her tone was almost arch.

'You're happy with John, aren't you?'

'Yes. And you know it. Did you ever resent me marrying again?'

'Far from it, Mamma. You know that, too.'

'Paul will be going to nursery school soon, I expect.'

'He can nearly read already,' Emma answered proudly. 'But thank Nanny for that as well as me.'

A great bowl of daffodils was reflected in polished wood, and another shone against the russet curtains.

Emma, deflected from her own affairs, admired them.

'They came from our garden. Oh, I forgot – you didn't know. John has bought us a country cottage near Angmering, about two miles from the sea. If you brought Paul down one week-end, we could take him on the beach. I know he's never seen the sea before.'

'He will cry "Thalassa! Thalassa!" I shall teach him,' Emma laughed. 'Yes, we'd love to come and do that.'

The men came in. Emma told Alan about the cottage, and about Paul going to see the sea. 'Have you two been talking politics, or swapping anecdotes not fit for our ears?'

'The former,' said John Winter. 'We were discussing the potential menace of Hitler.'

'And drinking Cockburn '27 port,' Alan said, 'a great treat.'

'What will you have now?' Winter asked. 'Brandy? Or something else?'

'I won't drink anything more, thank you. I have to drive.'

'Emma?'

'I'd like a whisky, please. Not too strong.'

'Whisky! You? You always drink gin,' said Agnes. 'I remember giving you your first gin and it, and feeling horribly guilty about it.'

'Well, I haven't gone to the devil, Mamma. But I've changed my ways.'

Alan said, 'Would you think me very impertinent, Mrs Winter, if I told you you were very pretty? You'll put Emma in the shade.' He gave her his charming smile.

'No,' she replied, 'I don't mind being told. But Emma has much better bones than I have.'

'I can't join in all this,' said Winter, returning with the drinks, 'only concur. Darling, what will you have?'

But Agnes, like Alan, would have nothing. She and Winter said good-bye to him cordially and hoped that he would come again.

'But I'm going to take Emma to see my house next Saturday, and it would be nice, Mrs Winter, if you came, too. You could give us your advice.'

So it was agreed that Agnes and Emma should both go.

But, during that week, Alan brought Emma a present. 'At least, it will be a present for you, but I shall keep him for the moment as he'd only be a bother to you.'

From the back of the car he produced a Sealyham puppy, perhaps two months old. He was a beautiful little animal, well bred, with fine rectangular head and tail turned up. He stood neatly on his points. 'Kim, this is your new mistress.'

'Oh, I'd love Paul to see him,' Emma cried. 'He's in bed, but I'll get him up for once.'

She went out, and returned bringing the little boy in his pyjamas and dressing-gown. 'This is Kim,' she said, 'and you must pat him very gently.'

The child was enchanted. 'Put out your hand to him first, old boy,' said Alan, 'and let him smell it. Then he can be sure you're friends.'

'Is he going to live here?'

'No, because he'd be too much trouble to Nanny. But he'll be with us when we get into our new house.'

'Does he like the deer?'

'We don't know yet. He may be frightened of them.'

'I believe he's as brave as brave,' said Paul. 'Why do you call him Kim?'

'After a boy in a book that you'll read some day.'

'It's a nice name.' He yawned.

'Back to bed with you, love. You can hardly keep your eyes open.'

'But I want to play with Kim!'

'You'll have plenty of time to do that.'

When he was back in bed, Alan said to Emma, 'I've something else for you.' He took from his pocket a jeweller's box and gave it to her.

She opened it and exclaimed. It held a square-cut emerald in a claw setting with shoulders of diamond chips. 'Oh, Alan, it's wonderful!'

Taking it from her, he put the ring on her finger. 'There. Now you can't escape me.' He kissed her. 'Are you sure you like it?'

' "Like" isn't the word. I adore it. Thank you! I can't wait to show people.' She was excited. 'I must call Nanny.'

'Tell her to come in and see Kim, too. I hope she likes dogs.'

Nanny came and was shown both ring and pup. She flushed with admiration of the ring, welcomed Kim, who jumped on her lap and curled up there.

'You can't stay there,' she said. 'I've got work to do.'

'Oh, forget about that,' said Emma. 'This is a very, very special evening. You must have a drink with us.'

So Nanny sipped at a glass of sherry. 'I'm sure I wish you both all happiness,' she said. 'Whatever will Paul have to say about this little fellow?'

'He's seen him,' said Emma. 'I let him get up for the purpose. He loved him. Don't scold me. I know I shouldn't have done it. But he wasn't asleep anyway. I think he is now.' She added, as if she could never come to an end of her good news, 'He's going to the sea soon. My mother's got a week-end cottage, and I'm taking Paul there. I wonder what he'll say when he sees it?'

'Small boys always know just what to do to the sea,' said Nanny unexpectedly. 'They throw stones at it.'

117

'And so shall he throw stones,' said Alan. 'I'll teach him to make them skip, when I take him to the seaside.'

'I'm so happy tonight,' Emma exclaimed. She was now wearing Stephen's ring on her right hand. She was never going to take it off.

'I'm sure you should be, M'm,' said Nanny, 'with such a beautiful ring and such a nice little dog. My, what whiskers he's got! My sister's got a fox-terrier; he's called Spot. He leads us both a dance, running away everywhere, and so hard to get back.' She put down her half-finished sherry, put Kim from her lap and wished them good-night.

'I've taken a great fancy to Nanny,' said Alan when she had gone. 'She's a great asset. And she's pretty sharp, too.'

When they called to pick up Agnes on the Saturday, Emma displayed her ring. 'I never saw anything so lovely!' Agnes said.

Alan drove them to see his house. It was a good-sized neo-Georgian one, almost adjacent to one of the park gates, and set back a little from the road. There was a small front garden with daffodils and, Alan said, a sizeable garden behind. His aunt Daisy was waiting with Kim to welcome them. Kim romped about them all.

Daisy was a spare little woman of seventy, sprightly, straight-backed, showing nothing of the rheumatic troubles of old age.

She welcomed Emma with a kiss. 'It's good to see you at last, and you, Mrs Winter. Come on in.'

They went in to warmth, although the day was not cold.

'Lunch will be ready in five minutes,' Daisy said, 'so help yourselves to drinks.' She left the room and Kim followed her.

'She'll be the one he's going to miss,' Emma said regretfully. 'What a pity there aren't two pups, one for Australia.'

The meal was a light one, consisting of a cheese soufflé, a salad and a raspberry tart. 'Frozen,' Daisy said, 'but I think it's edible.'

After the meal they went for a tour of the house. It had four large bedrooms, two with bath attached. 'This one', Daisy said, opening a door, 'is mine. When I go I thought it might do for your nanny and Paul. I'm longing to see him.'

Emma said, 'It would do splendidly, if it didn't mean turning you out.'

'But I'm going out anyway, my dear. It will be helpful having the bathroom handy, I think. And there's a little pantry up here where Nanny could make his food and tea for herself. Nannies always drink tea. – This will be yours and Alan's room.' This, too, was large, and had a four-poster bed. 'There is another bath along the passage, besides yours.'

'It is all splendid,' said Emma, and Agnes agreed.

'And here's a guest-room, and here's another for a housekeeper. You'll need that.'

'But I'm sure I can manage—'

'It's a big house, Emma dear. Better not try. Well, will you want to see the kitchen?'

'I'd like to,' Agnes said, 'if I might.'

This, again, was large, equipped with a refrigerator and a double sink unit. 'There's a good bit of walking-about in here,' said Daisy, 'but I don't like skimpy kitchens.'

When the tour of inspection was finished, they went down into the drawing-room, which ran from end to end of the house and was consequently sunny. 'There's the garden.' Daisy pointed through the back window. 'It's mostly flowering shrubs and a rockery, so it's not all that much work. We have a man in twice a week and he copes with it easily. Oh, my dear,' she said to Emma, 'you can't think how good it is to meet you. I hope Alan's going to be very kind to you.'

'As kind as I know how,' he said. 'And I make that promise to Mrs Winter, too.'

'It seems to me that, as we're going to be related, you'd better call me Agnes.'

'I'm honoured,' he said. 'Emma, I'm going to take you round the garden, so put your coat on.'

It was nothing more than a rectangular piece of ground, covering about a third of an acre, but had been so cunningly landscaped with winding paths and irregular-shaped flowerbeds that it looked luxurious. There was prunus and cherryblossom. 'Well, do you like it?'

'I love it,' said Emma, 'and I love your aunt Daisy. I'm sorry you're going to lose her.'

'She always said she wouldn't stay when this place had a mistress. Can you see yourself in that role?'

'I can but try. Oh dear,' she added, 'and I never showed her my ring!'

'To tell you the truth, I showed it to her first to see whether she thought you would like it. She did think so.'

'And she was right.'

They returned to Agnes and Daisy, who were just finishing their coffee. 'Well, I think we'd better be going,' Alan said, 'if we're going to get you back in good time.'

Daisy kissed both Emma and Agnes on their leaving. 'It has been nice having you here. I hope to see you again before the great event.'

They thanked her as warmly and went away.

Agnes said in the car, 'Emma, you're a lucky girl.'

'I hope she'll turn out to be. It won't be for the want of trying.'

'It's a lovely house.'

'And there will be the garden for Paul,' he said, 'though I hope he's not still going on calling me "Mr Beasht".'

'I'll spank him if he does,' said Emma, 'and it will be for the first time.'

Chapter Six

THEY were married very quietly at Chelsea Old Church. Jack Hamer, a golfing friend of Alan's, was best man; John Winter gave Emma away. Aunt Daisy was there. Sylvia was present at her own request ('You'll ask me, sweetie? You know I wish you well'). Alan, treating her as a bridesmaid, gave her a gold and enamel bracelet. They drank champagne at Emma's flat, and afterwards went to lunch at the Savoy.

Then they went off on a ten-day honeymoon, to Venice, Emma not caring to leave Paul for longer. They were not to make the move into Alan's house until they came back, fearing the disturbance of the move in their absence would upset Paul. Alan had put the wedding announcement in both *The Times* and the *Telegraph*. This gave their anonymous letter-writer all the facts she needed, and when they returned to the flat Emma hastily swept up the familiar postcard and put it in her hand-bag. This time she would show it to Alan. But she did not read it that day.

She was thunderstruck by the beauty of Venice and, when she caught her first sight of the Piazza San Marco, thanked Alan for giving her such wonderful things to see. Good-humouredly, he let himself be dragged from museum to museum, church to church. She was rapt with wonder.

In bed he appeased her longings, though he did not rival Stephen's preliminary play. He was too eager to get on with the job.

They rowed in gondolas, visited Torbello by motor-boat, dined at a restaurant near the Fenice, under roofing vines and by candlelight. They walked and walked. Emma wondered why her feet were so sore. 'Well, you must have done about eight miles today, my girl. Let's go and have a drink.' They drank negronis at the Cavalletto, where they were staying, and afterwards had a bottle of heavy Barolo with their dinner.

Afterwards, emboldened by the wine, she showed Alan the postcard she had hidden, and told him of the history of this persecution. It read:

SO YOU'VE CAUGHT ANOTHER ONE, HA HA. YOU AND GIDDY MAMMA ARE GOOD AT MARRYING. TELL HIM TO BE GOOD TO YOU AND THE BRAT OR I'LL BEAT THE LIFE OUT OF HIM.

'This must go to the police,' Alan said.

'We took the others to the police, but they were no good.'

'Have you any idea who it is?'

'Not the slightest. The police thought it was a woman, but I'm not so sure.'

'Well, if you get another of these don't read it, but give it to me. Will you promise?'

'I think I can promise, but they have a hideous fascination.'

He put the card in his pocket. 'We'll forget about this. Are you too tired, or shall we go to the Piazza? There's a concert on there tonight. Didn't you see them putting up the stands?'

She said she was not too tired. They went out into the full moonlight, where St Mark's looked like something out of a fairy tale, and listened a trifle half-heartedly to the band. Between the cafés scores of Venetians roamed the night, pausing to have their concert free. Alan drank a glass of white wine and Emma had a granitá. 'This is heaven,' she said.

'You're happy?'

'Very.'

'No regrets?'

'None.'

'I'll save you from them. Will you forget that beastly post-card, now I've taken it over?'

'I've forgotten, for the moment.'

When they got back to England, Emma returned, as arranged, to the flat. It would take her two days to prepare for the move to her new home. Nanny helped her with her clothes and Paul's. Emma was taking only one thing with her, the piano, besides Paul's toys. He had been very good in her absence, though he had constantly asked when she was coming home. He insisted on taking his alphabet bricks. 'I can spell lots of things out now,' he said.

'That he can,' Nanny confirmed. 'He writes, "Mummy is now called Mrs Priest." I taught him.'

'I shall have to pay you an extra salary as a governess, at this rate.'

The move went off without any difficulty and Emma found that Daisy had done marvels. She had converted one of the spare rooms into a day nursery for Paul, and to welcome him had bought him a set of Beatrix Potter books. These he received with delight, and wanted Nanny to read to him at once. He was pleased to have his bed in her room, and jumped on it to show his joy. Kim came to play with his rubber bone. 'You must be careful not to take it away from him until he puts it down,' Alan said. 'He thinks it's a real bone anyway.'

'I'll be very careful,' Paul said. 'When can I see the deer?'

'Well, not today,' Emma began. 'There's so much to do—'

'I'll take him this afternoon,' said Alan. 'There's very little to do as far as I'm concerned.'

'Go with Papa?' Paul had learned one of his lessons. 'That's good. And take Kim, too.'

'Come out in the garden now, and see all the flowers,' said Daisy. 'Then you must all meet Mrs Stewart, who's going to be your cook-housekeeper.'

She appeared to announce luncheon. She was a stout, pretty woman of about forty-five, and looked pleased as she greeted Emma.

'I hope I'll suit, Madam.'

'I'm sure you will.'

Daisy had bought Paul a high-chair, and he sat at table with them. The food was excellent. Paul, impressed by his surroundings, ate without messiness. 'Isn't he a good boy?' Daisy exclaimed.

'He's on his best behaviour today,' said Emma. 'I hope he keeps it up.'

'More pudding,' said Paul, adding 'Please.'

He had been once to Angmering and, as Nanny had predicted, had immediately started to throw stones at the sea. He had wanted to go a second time, but Emma had realised that Alan did not care for her to be away for a week-end. But later on they would take him to Angmering, too.

Emma went to bed by Alan's side tired out. It had been such a busy day, even with Nanny's help, unpacking and getting everything in order. Paul had been uncharacteristically fretful at bedtime, having realised that he really was not going to sleep with Mummy. Emma did her best to soothe him, singing from her now enlarged repertoire as he sat on his pot. She asked him how he had liked the deer, and he brightened. But he was more charmed by a walk through the thick bracken, which was high enough to close over his head. 'Will you like it here?' Emma asked him. He thought so. He made her read to him from Beatrix Potter for a while. 'I will be able to read that soon,' he said.

He was sent to a nursery school, only a hundred yards away down the road. There were no scenes as Emma left him. He was fascinated by the other children and by the teachers. He was to be taught by Miss Dawlish, he said afterwards.

He settled in comfortably for a while until, one day, weeping, he refused to go to school. 'But why?' asked Emma. 'You've been so happy there.'

'Not go to school.'

But she dressed him and led him there, almost having to drag him. At one moment he escaped her and hid behind a privet hedge in a front garden. She stared around her, puzzled, unable to see what was frightening him. There was nobody in sight but a girl of eighteen or nineteen.

She forced him out from behind the hedge, whereupon he sat down on the pavement. 'What is it? You must tell me.'

'Miss Dawlish. There she is.'

He pointed to the girl. 'She put me in the corner.' And he burst into tears. 'She's cruel.'

'I'll go right into the school with you and put things right.'

But still she had to drag him.

She went straight to the headmistress. 'Paul's upset about Miss Dawlish. She made him stand in the corner. Why?'

'I can tell you why, Mrs Priest. Paul's a chatterbox, and that was the only way she could keep him quiet.'

'By humiliating him? I wouldn't have minded her giving him a smart smack on the leg.'

'We don't approve of corporal punishment, not in any school.'

'It is never to happen again. He was so happy, and now he's miserable.'

The headmistress rang a bell and an assistant appeared. 'Go and ask Miss Dawlish if she can spare me a few minutes.'

They waited. Then the girl came in, much flustered. She looked absurdly young to be counted as a 'teacher' by Paul.

'This is Mrs Priest. She's complaining because you put Paul in the corner.'

'The other children laughed at him,' said Emma. 'He couldn't bear that.'

'I couldn't stop him talking any other way. He was disrupting the class,' Miss Dawlish said, rather grandly.

'I'd rather you'd smacked him.'

'We're not allowed to do that here.'

'Anyway, he must never go in the corner again.'

'If he doesn't chatter any more, he won't,' said the headmistress.

'No. Whatever he does, it must never happen again, or else I shall take him away.'

'We'll see.'

'We won't see,' said Emma. 'We will make sure.'

'Other children don't mind,' Miss Dawlish said tentatively. 'They don't mind a bit.'

'Then why use it as a punishment?'

The girl was silent, a slow flush rising up her neck to her forehead. 'Promise me it won't happen again,' said Emma.

'Are you able to promise that?' said the headmistress, in an effort to uphold her staff. 'Can you make sure he doesn't chatter again?'

'I don't think he will,' said Emma and, satisfied, took her leave. Next morning, when she took Paul to school, she found he had been moved into another form. 'I hope the other teacher will be kind,' he said.

Alan and Emma had been married for about three months when she became vaguely worried that he was drinking too much. When he came home from work, the first thing he did was to go to the drinks cupboard. He usually had two stiff whiskies before dinner, and three or more before bedtime. She never saw him drunk and supposed he had a great tolerance for alcohol.

Then, one day towards the end of August, he took time from the office to play a foursome of golf with Jack Hamer and two friends. It was seven o'clock before he came home and she heard his key fumbling in the lock. Paul was playing with Kim before bedtime, and was in his pyjamas and dressing-gown. 'Hullo, young sir,' said Alan, ruffling his hair. He kissed Emma. 'All go well today?'

'Fine. Mrs Stewart has made you a curry for dinner. I remember that you liked it.'

'If it's anything like as good as yours, I do.' He poured himself a drink, offered one to her, which she accepted. She had read her Ibsen and believed that, like Mrs Alving, she could restrain him. It was a warm night. He had taken off his coat and pullover and was sitting in his shirt and plus-fours.

Paul was still playing with Kim and his bone. He must have pulled it away too sharply, because the dog snapped at him. Alan stood up. 'I'll soon stop that sort of thing,' he said. 'Snap once and he'll bite next. He's old enough to learn.'

To Emma's horror he snatched up the lead from a window sill and began to thrash the dog, who whimpered and cowered.

'Please stop,' she said. Paul burst into a storm of tears.

'Never too young to learn. And take that brat away!'

Emma said to Paul, 'Go to Nanny now. I'll see you later.'

'But Papa's hitting Kim!'

'Kim snapped at you. And Papa's not really hurting him.'

'He is, he is!' She took Paul up to Nanny, hastened down again. Alan was still punishing the dog, who was crawling on his stomach.

'If you don't stop that, I'll leave you!'

In surprise, he let go of the lead, which Emma snatched away.

'You'll do what?'

'I'll leave you, if you ever do that again. I can't bear it.'

The dog crawled away under the valance of an armchair.

Alan came to her, his face very red. 'It was only because he snapped at Paul. We can't have that sort of thing happening again. Listen, old girl, Kim's not hurt much. You'll see.'

'And you called Paul a brat.'

He tried to embrace her. 'I'm sorry. I'm afraid I'm a bit the worse for wear. I'll go up to wash and change. Tell Mrs Stewart to keep dinner for a quarter of an hour.'

As he left the room, she began to tremble. The scene had been too much for her, and she was hard put to it not to cry. But she went to speak to Mrs Stewart and then to say good-night to Paul. She found the child still shaking and blubbering, with Nanny trying to soothe him. 'Papa whipped Kim.'

'Hush. It was only because Kim snapped at you. Papa's sorry now.'

Between them, they succeeded in comforting him, even giving him a sweet, which he was not usually allowed to have after he had cleaned his teeth.

Emma returned to the drawing-room, where Alan sat subdued. He said at once, 'I'm sorry to have upset you, darling. But I couldn't bear to see Kim snapping at Paul.'

'It was only a playful snap. You were cruel.'

'I didn't mean to be. I'd had a long day.'

'So I could see. And a long evening in the bar.'

'It was only once in a way. Jack and I won and we had to celebrate.'

The dog came out from under the armchair and went to him. 'You see? He doesn't bear malice.' Alan patted him. 'You're all right, aren't you? I told you he wasn't much hurt. You didn't mean that about leaving me?'

'I did, if it ever happens again.'

'It won't.'

He had recovered himself sufficiently to make a pretence of eating the curry, though Emma saw that he could scarcely bring himself to do so. He did not drink again that night and could not touch her when they went to bed.

The breach, of course, was soon healed, though Emma knew that she had given Alan a shock. He seemed to be drinking less, at least, when she saw him, and she was hopeful for the future. 'I wish we could have a child of our own,' he said one day. She, too, wished it, but they had had no luck. She thought of consulting a doctor. 'But it might be my fault,' he said. 'I'd better see my man, too.'

It transpired that both of them were fertile. 'So we can only wait and hope,' Alan said. 'Paul would like a brother or sister.'

But Emma was not so sure.

Chapter Seven

AGNES came to lunch once a week, driving the little car that Winter had given her. She drove competently, as she did all things. This day she and Emma walked in the garden, where Paul was playing with Kim. He was too wary to use the bone again, but threw the dog a ball.

'He's a fine boy,' Agnes said as she watched him. 'But what's the matter with you, darling? You're looking rather pale. Surely you get enough fresh air?'

'Do I? I feel all right. Yes, I get ample fresh air. Alan's teaching me to play golf. I'm not bad. The walking tires me rather, and I only do nine holes.'

The garden was looking beautiful, with michaelmas daisies and golden rod, the latter high enough to hide Paul completely. The trees were showing all their autumn colours.

'You're not,' her mother began tentatively, 'you're not expecting?'

'I am not, worse luck. I'd like another, and so would Alan.' But Emma did not really care. Ever since the incident of the dog, her feeling for Alan had cooled, not completely, but sufficiently to worry her. She had even begun to feel wicked that she had married him without really loving him completely, and knew she must atone for this for the rest of her life. Yet he was very kind to her and Paul, though Paul would not, even now, go to him without reluctance and she knew that this irked him. So she played golf or walked the course with him, and entertained his friends. At these parties his drinking was moderate and he seemed to restrain himself, making a glass of whisky last a long time. The sound of his key in the latch did not give her the excitement that Stephen's had done.

The Hoods had come to visit them. Sylvia was now engaged, and Noel, after three months doing all manner of odd jobs, had gone up to Oxford. The older Hoods were easy with Emma and Alan, and did not show their regrets.

The little boy ran gleefully out of the golden rod, and Emma swept him up into her arms. Agnes hugged him, too. 'Do you still love Granny?'

'Yes,' he replied, 'I love Granny. And Mummy, and Nanny.' He wriggled down. Kim came up, standing on his points, his tail erect. 'Love Kim, too.' He began again to throw the ball, delighted when the dog brought it back and put it at his feet.

'I can really read now,' he told Agnes proudly.

'He's forward, isn't he?' she said. 'How's he doing at school?'

Splendidly, Emma replied. He could recite up to his four-times tables, too.

'Was Stephen clever as a child?'

'Not all that much. And nor was I, so I don't know where Paul gets it from.'

Mrs Stewart came out to tell them that lunch was ready. 'I've made some minced chicken for Paul.' Nanny Harcourt was on a week's holiday at her home.

When the meal was over and Paul had been put down for his sleep, Agnes reverted to Emma's appearance. 'You are pale. You're not worrying about anything?'

'Why should I, Mamma? Everything's fine and Paul's flourishing.'

'Oh, I meant to tell you! Poor Polly's dead. We found her on the bottom of her cage. I shall miss her.'

'I expect you will.' Emma would not speak ill of the dead.

'We buried her in the garden and John made a little cross out of two pieces of wood.'

'She was very old.'

'I expect she was, but she was so perky that it came as a shock.'

'I know how I would feel if it was Kim. I'm very sorry.'

But Agnes, who had only been diverted for the moment, continued to watch her daughter with a doubtful eye. 'Did Paul enjoy his holiday?' They had taken him and Nanny to

Lyme Regis.

'He did indeed. He wanted to paddle all day. Alan built him sandcastles, but all he really cared about was paddling.'

'And you?'

'When it was warm I swam a little. Alan doesn't swim.'

'Nor did your father. But John's a strong swimmer. I'm always afraid he'll go out too far.'

Alan came in early. It was Saturday. He kissed Agnes.

'I've been playing tennis. But I shan't do much more now. I'm getting too old to run about. How are you?'

'I'm all right. But I think Emma is peaky.'

He tilted his wife's face. 'I don't think she is.'

'I must use more make-up,' said Emma.

'You haven't a mother's sharp eye,' Agnes said.

'Perhaps I haven't. She looks good to me.' He added, 'How's Paul?'

'Sleeping the sleep of the just,' Emma replied. 'Who won?'

'We were playing singles. I lost.'

'You'll win next time,' Agnes said comfortably.

'Have you had lunch?' Emma asked.

'At the club. Cold meat.'

'Paul's been in the garden all the morning. Playing with Kim.'

Kim was asleep on a cushion. 'Good,' said Alan. He asked after Agnes and Winter. 'I see you're driving your own car.'

'Yes, it's a great comfort.'

They passed a pleasant enough afternoon. Paul came down and Agnes read to him. 'But I can read "Mrs Tiggy-Winkle,"' he protested. 'Let's try "Squirrel Nutkin". That's my favourite.'

'You and John must come to dinner soon. Lunch is usually sparse,' Alan said. 'We'll give you something more substantial.'

'I can't run about as I used to do,' he said when Agnes had gone. 'I shall take up shooting again.' His guns were in a cupboard in the hall. He added, 'Pigeons and rabbits. But savoury.'

Hitler had become Chancellor, and Alan was perturbed.

131

'He's going too fast, too far,' he said.

Emma agreed. He had taught her to take an interest in politics.

'All the same,' he said, 'you can't say he isn't making something out of that benighted country. He must get the credit for that.'

'By taking away all its liberties, so far as I can see,' said Emma.

'You can't make an omelette without breaking eggs. Well, I'm a bit tired. I'm going to have a lie-down. Don't wake me for tea.' He slept till nearly five.

She took Paul for a walk in the park. 'Papa peeped in at me,' he said. 'I always know.'

'You always know most things, it seems to me.'

'Oh, no,' he said, 'not my five-times yet.'

'But that's an easy one. I'll teach you.'

'Now?'

'If you like.'

'No, thank you, I'd rather play.' Kim was with them and they had brought his ball.

'Be careful not to send it into the bracken,' Emma said, 'or he'll never find it again.'

That evening they were to go to dinner with the Hamers, who had a house by Wimbledon Common.

'What shall I wear?' she asked Alan, who liked to be consulted.

'Your green,' he replied promptly. 'And I like your hair that way.' She now wore it straight to where it curled under at the ends.

'We've just time for bed,' he suggested.

'Oh, not now! It'll be such a rush, and we'll be late.'

He said no more, but got on with his dressing.

The Hamers were rather loud, cheerful people who liked to drink. Alan kept up with them. Dinner was a long and elaborate meal, cooked by Mrs Hamer herself. Afterwards the men and women did not separate, but drank port in the drawing-room.

'What a pretty dress, Emma,' Mrs Hamer said, 'and you're looking very pretty, too.'

'It's only an old thing,' Emma answered, confused, 'but Alan likes it.'

'And so he might! I'm glad to hear that he knows what you're wearing. Jack never pays attention to my clothes.'

They stayed late. When at last they drove away, Alan was unexpectedly quarrelsome. 'Why can't you take a compliment gracefully? It's no good snubbing people who mean to be kind.'

'I didn't snub her.'

'Well, it sounded like it.'

She cried out, 'Alan! You cut that corner close!'

'Don't you become a back–seat driver. I know my own business.' But his driving was erratic.

However, they got back safely and when they did so his black mood had disappeared. 'We'll have a nightcap,' he said. 'Might as well be hanged for a sheep as a lamb.'

She tried to expostulate, but saw that it was no good. She had a last drink with him, hoping to hurry him up. He sat with his till past midnight.

When at last they were in bed he said, 'I'm going to beget that kid, as the Bible says. Move farther over.'

Even now she wanted him, her body as hungry as ever. But it was no good. He could not take her that night. After a long time of panting and straining he rolled off her and on to his back. 'Sorry, old girl. I'm just too tired, I expect. Another time.' He went to sleep almost at once. Emma lay awake, deprived and worrying. He had never failed before. She knew he was drinking too much, not steadily, but in bouts. What was she to do? She believed that this was her own punishment. She thought of Denzil, whose last name she had never known, and about that solitary night of easement. She was being punished for that, too. She wished God had not made her so sexually hungry.

Alan. How many people had noticed? Mrs Stewart, when he sometimes rejected her meals? Nanny, who often spent an hour or two in the drawing-room sewing, and listening to the wireless. Alan with his eternal glass in hand, though always courteous. Nanny, she fancied, saw most things, and she had begun to notice that her visits to the drawing-room, despite invitation, were becoming fewer. Emma's Sundays on the links were calming for a while, though she dreaded the visit to the club-house afterwards. She now played all eighteen holes, and enjoyed the game. But when they came home for a late lunch, there was Alan's erratic appetite to be feared. Sometimes he would eat a good deal, at other times not at all. On Saturdays he preferred shooting, and came back with a few pigeons which Mrs Stewart had to dress and put into a pie. 'Old hand hasn't lost its cunning,' he had said.

She drifted into an uneasy sleep, and dreamed that Denzil was playing golf with her, saying that it all took too long and that he wanted to go to the 'nineteenth hole' for a drink.

When she awoke she was calm. Alan still slept heavily. She put on her dressing-gown and went to Paul.

'He's eaten his breakfast,' Nanny said. 'Wolfed every bit of it. Some prunes, an egg and a piece of fried bread. And a glass of milk.'

'I'm not hungry now, Mummy,' said Paul. 'Nanny gave me breakfast.'

'Why, is it late?'

'A quarter to ten, M'm. Mrs Stewart wants to know when you and Mr Priest will be coming down.'

'I'll come as I am. Mr Priest will be sleeping late.'

She was ravenously hungry. She 'wolfed' her breakfast, as Nanny would have said, and then smoked three cigarettes. She was just wondering whether she should awaken Alan when she heard him coming downstairs. He was fully dressed and looked fresh. 'Will you have something?' she asked.

'Of course I will. Finished, have you? I'm sorry to put Mrs Stewart to extra trouble.'

'No trouble at all, sir,' said Mrs Stewart, coming in for orders. 'What will you have?'

'What did my wife have? Kidneys? They'll do for me.'

'I didn't,' said Emma, 'but there are some.'

When they were alone he said, 'Sorry I overslept. Sorry about last night. I don't know what got into me.'

'I do,' she said boldly. 'Drink.'

'Oh, come, come, I hadn't had that much. No, I was just unaccountably fagged.'

So she said no more.

One day they had a surprise visit from Eric Flowers. He was engaged, he said, to one of Mr Cochran's Young Ladies. 'Her name's Rosemary.'

'Pretty,' said Emma. They gave him their congratulations.

'Of course, she's a good bit younger than me. I'm only an old bachelor.' And, indeed, they saw that he had had his hair and moustache dyed. He wore white flannel trousers and a navy-blue blazer with brass buttons.

'How's Agnes?' he asked. 'Sprightly as ever?'

'As ever,' Emma replied.

He would not stay for dinner, though they tried to persuade him. He had had several drinks to keep Alan company, and said that he didn't dare have any more lest they should impair his driving. They thought him a nice little man and Emma told Alan how he had once lent her his bungalow. 'He's always after young girls,' she said, 'and I hope this is the one for him.'

'I shouldn't have thought he was quite the thing for a Cochran's Young Lady.'

'Nor should I. But you never know. Tastes differ.'

'I'll say they do,' he said. 'He can't mean to take her to live in a dripping-wet bungalow?'

'Perhaps he doesn't. He's got lots of money.'

'And she'll have lots of rheumatism if he does. That will stop her dancing.'

'Oh, don't be malicious, Alan. It's not like you.'

'I wasn't being. Simply making a practical observation.'

'Mamma will be interested.'

'Your mamma's interested in everything. That's what I like about her.'

'You do like her?'

'Of course I do. And if you look like her when you're her age you won't be doing so badly.'

So they got along. Her golfing pleased him, and he was glad to have made cautious friends again with Paul. He was rarely so quarrelsome again, and she fancied that he was making amends for the past.

Chapter Eight

THE annual club-dance was held early in December. Alan urged Emma to invite her mother and step-father. 'They like dancing, don't they? Anyway, it's a lively affair.' They accepted, and he was pleased. He liked them both.

Emma and Agnes had both bought new dresses for the occasion. Emma's was white, Agnes's blue. The club-house was lavishly decorated for the occasion, in anticipation of Christmas. There were balloons hanging from the ceiling. Alan settled the four of them in a corner and brought them drinks. The weatherbeaten women were there, and a number of young ones with their men friends. Dancing had already begun. John Winter invited Emma on to the floor, and Alan took Agnes, explaining that he was rusty and couldn't live up to her standards. 'I'm all feet,' he said, 'but I'll do my best not to step on yours.'

Winter told Emma how kind it was of her to have invited them. 'We don't go to many festive occasions these days,' he said, 'though we do dance occasionally.' He danced well, and she felt inferior to him; she had danced little since Stephen died. The noise-level was high, and they had to shout to hear each other.

Alan danced once with Emma, and then seemed content to sit in the corner drinking. She hoped and prayed that it would not be too much.

Several men whom she knew invited her to dance. Jack Hamer was there with his bouncy wife, and they invited her to sit with them. 'This is jolly,' Hamer said. 'We haven't all met since the wedding. That was jolly, too.'

He took their orders for another round. Agnes and John did not accept, but Emma said she would have a Pimm's No.1. She wanted to keep up with Alan so far as she could, thinking he would attract less attention if he did not drink alone.

'"Blue skies, smiling at me,"' the band sang. '"Nothing but blue skies do I see."'

'That's a pretty old one,' Alan said.

'I like the old ones,' said Mrs Hamer. 'When you're my age you like to be reminded of things. We used to dance to that.'

'Dance with me,' said Alan. She got up. He rose, too, and staggered a little. Emma went cold. 'Caught my foot,' he said, though there was nothing for him to catch it in.

Nevertheless, he seemed to be dancing steadily enough and Emma's fears subsided. Perhaps he had genuinely caught his foot, or it had gone to sleep while he had been sitting down. After all, he had had only the one drink before they left the house.

In another half-hour the band struck up a Paul Jones.

'Everybody in this,' Hamer cried, 'girls in the middle, men outside.'

Alan had slumped a little in his chair. 'Count me out.'

'No, we won't. You're coming, too.'

Alan obeyed. He joined the outer circle with John and Hamer, while Agnes and Emma linked hands in the middle.

The music began, and the dancers began to circle. Emma stopped in front of a tall man whom she did not know. She could not see Alan over his shoulder. 'Cherry do,' the man said. They were back in their circles again. Emma was left out this time and went gratefully back to her chair. Agnes was dancing with the club secretary, Winter with a very young girl. Alan, seeming steady, had been claimed by the secretary's daughter. The music stopped. The circling began again. Emma did not join it. Stop. Alan was opposite a stout woman, who was an excellent golfer. A waltz this time. Emma saw him swing her round with a kind of exuberance. He looked nimble enough.

Then it happened. He tripped and fell heavily to the ground, bearing the woman with him. The dancing stopped. John and Emma went to him, and so did several of the women.

'Dora, are you all right?'

'I wasn't hurt. I'm afraid I fell on Mr Priest.'

It took Winter, Hamer and two other men to get Alan to his feet. He was looking white and dazed. 'Sorry,' he said, 'very sorry. My foot turned.'

Shrugging off assistance, he weaved his way back to his chair. 'Bring me a scotch,' he said to Hamer. 'I could do with it.'

'Are you sure you could, old boy?'

'I've told you.'

'Better get off home,' Winter said. 'I'll drive you, Alan. You've had a heavy fall.'

'Can drive myself.'

'I'm not going to let you. Agnes, you can bring Emma. There's been enough dancing tonight.'

Alan protested violently, but Winter was firm. 'A fall like that is always a shock. Come on.'

Agnes and Emma saw him helped into the car, and Winter groped for the keys.

'So you see,' said Emma.

'I see,' Agnes replied. 'Is it often like this?'

'Not so bad. He's never fallen before.'

'What are we going to do about it?'

'There's nothing to do whatsoever. I'm sorry your evening was spoiled.'

'Oh, *that*! We'll see him right into the house. Does anyone know?'

'I expect several of the men at the club do. It's hard to conceal and of course he drinks more when he's not with me. If he is, he really tries.'

Emma felt a sense of relief in so confiding to her mother to whom, this time, she could hardly keep quiet. It was as though a share in the burden had been lifted from her.

When they reached the house, Winter and Alan were on the doorstep. 'He can't find his keys,' Winter said.

'I've got mine,' said Emma. She gave it to him. They all went into the house.

Alan said with a silly grin, 'How about a nightcap?'

'No,' she replied firmly, 'you're going straight up.'

'Don't know that I can make it, old girl.'

'John will help.'

They had got him half-way up the flight when he fell flat on his face and slid down three steps. This time he was beyond speech, and none of them could get him to his feet.

138

'We can't leave him there!' Emma cried out. She was by now half-hysterical.

'I can drag him down the rest of the way, so that he lies flat. Then we can get a pillow and something to cover him up. He'll sleep it off in half an hour.' John dragged at Alan's feet, succeeded in getting him to the floor of the hall. He fetched a cushion from the drawing-room and covered him with his own overcoat. Alan slept.

'You'd better both go now,' Emma said. 'It must be terribly late.'

'Only half past eleven,' said Agnes, 'and we're not going till we know you're all right.' They went back into the drawing-room, leaving Alan to his sleep, and for nearly an hour they spoke little. Then they heard noises from the hall. He had woken up at last, and was making his way again up the stairs. They saw him right into the bedroom, where he lay down upon the bed. 'Lousy host,' he said. 'Thousand apologies. Don't know what came over me.' This was his usual excuse.

Agnes was crying when they left the house. 'My poor darling, how are you going to bear it?'

'I can bear it. Don't you worry about me. I'll get to bed now.'

Because he was lying half-sprawled across it, she had to turn the clothes back over him before she herself could get in at all. She neither removed her make-up nor washed her face, as she usually did at night, but lay down in a state of exhaustion and fell asleep at once.

She awoke at eight o'clock to find him, fully dressed, sitting at her side. He took her hand. 'I'm sorry about last night, darling. I overdid it. Who drove me home?'

'John did. And brought you in.'

'I found myself on the hall floor but I got up myself.'

'Yes.'

'Are you very angry with me?'

'No. Just depressed.'

'I'll be all right now, you'll see. Are you getting up?'

'No. Ask Mrs Stewart to bring me a cup of tea and some toast in bed.'

'Will do. Have you forgiven me?'

'Oh, of course I have. What's the use?'

'I promise you, things are going to get better. Was I very awful at the club?'

'You had a fall, you know. You weren't badly hurt, though.'

'While I was dancing? I don't remember much.'

'With Mrs Hutchinson.'

'Oh, Christ.'

'She wasn't hurt, either.'

He got up. 'Well, I'd better be going down. I could eat some breakfast myself. I'll look in on Paul.'

'Yes, do. Tell him I'll be with him soon.'

From that day on, however, he began to drink openly, no more concealment. Every night he had the bottle on a table at his side, plainly visible both to Nanny and to Mrs Stewart. Emma attempted gently to expostulate with him, but he merely told her not to nag. 'You're turning into a nagger, you know. I should never have thought it.' But he exhibited few symptoms of drunkenness except – it was rare – when he was sick just before bedtime and only partially flushed the vomit away. In the mornings he ate a good meal and left for the office on time, usually returning about seven in the evening.

Then, on New Year's Eve, he was very late. Nanny was with her sister, and it was Mrs Stewart's day off. Emma did not bother to eat much herself, and made no preparations for Alan. If he wanted anything when he got in, she would make it. She sat over coffee and cigarettes at the dinner-table and listened for his key. At last it came. It was past nine o'clock. She heard him come along the hall to the cloakroom, and then he seemed to go in search of something in the cupboard under the stairs. She heard him fumbling his way back to the drawing-room. When she joined him there, she had a shock.

He was sitting with that giggly look on his face, his shotgun across his knees. 'Sit down,' he said. 'I'm going to kill you. Before you nag again.'

She was terrified, but she kept her head. She said, 'You can't kill anyone with that, it's too dirty. If you give it to me, I'll clean it.' She held out her hands, and to her amazement he dropped the gun into them.

'Don't be long,' he said, 'because I'm going to kill you.'

She ran out of the room and upstairs to the telephone. She rang the doctor. 'Donald, come at once. Alan's very bad and he's threatening to shoot me. I'm scared.'

'Don't panic. I'll be with you in five minutes.'

She did not know how to clean a gun, but she did know how to unload it. There were cartridges in it, and these she dropped into a box in the cupboard. Then she returned to him. He was still grinning, and the bottle was still beside him. Shakily he poured himself a drink. Seeing the gun he said, 'Give me that.' She did so, and once more he laid it across his knees.

The doctor came and without a word took the gun away.

'Hey, what are you doing, Doc? That's mine.'

'I don't think you're well. I'd like to examine you.'

'As fit as a fiddle. I'm going to kill her. She nags, nag, nag, all the time.'

'You come upstairs. I want to take your blood-pressure.'

'Why?'

'Because I think it's going to be too low. Come along now; I'll help you up.'

And Alan meekly complied. 'A happy New Year,' he said, slurring his words. He let the doctor help him into the bedroom, and Emma followed.

'Now, take off your coat, and that pullover.' But this Alan could not manage, so the doctor did it for him. He still wore the same grin during the examination – heart, lungs and blood-pressure.

'You'll do,' the doctor said, 'though I want you to take some pills. I've got them here. Eight every night and morning. Now, you get into bed and don't get up in the morning. I'll call in on you early.'

It was all they could do to help Alan into his pyjamas and get him settled. 'Where's my gun?' he said.

'It's been put away. Try to get to sleep. And I warn you, if you have too many thick nights like this you'll go to sleep for good and all.'

For the first time, Alan looked frightened. 'Where's Emma? I want Emma.'

'Here I am.'

He fumbled for her hand. 'Didn't really mean to shoot you. Only to stop you nagging.'

'I won't nag you again. Go to sleep.'

'Are you coming?'

'When I've seen Donald out.'

'Good old Donald,' he said, and his eyes closed. 'Thinks I'm ill.'

When the doctor was satisfied that he was sleeping, he and Emma went downstairs. 'You could do with a drink yourself,' he said to her. 'His blood-pressure's right down and his pulse-rate's feeble.' He poured her a drink, accepted one for himself. 'Has he ever been like this before?'

'Never so bad.'

'You'll have to watch him. Ration his drinks if you can. I think I'd better get him into a home tomorrow. You can't possibly nurse him.'

'Perhaps you'd better,' she said. She was exhausted.

'Is there anyone in the house with you?'

'Only Paul. Nanny comes back in a couple of days, and Mrs Stewart will be late in tonight.'

'If he gives you any more trouble, ring me, however late it is. But I don't think he will. I'll be in by ten, and I hope to have fixed him up a bed by then. I'll take him there myself. His dressing-gown will do to go in, and you can pack a bag for him. Is there anywhere you can sleep by yourself tonight?'

'There's one of the spare rooms. But I can't leave him. He may wake up in the small hours and want me.'

'Well, I can't stop you. You're a brave girl, Emma. Braver than I should have been.'

She thanked him and he left her.

The house was very quiet. The gun lay on the sofa where the doctor had thrown it, and she took it back to the cupboard, where she turned the key and put it in her own bag.

It was now only a quarter to ten. She sat and waited, and for a while she dozed in her chair.

He slept heavily during the night and into the next day. A happy New Year, he had said. She cried a little, a rare luxury with her.

She left a note to tell Mrs Stewart that Mr Priest was ill, and not to bother about breakfast for him. He had seen the doctor and would stay in bed. She could imagine the expression on the woman's face, a 'That's as maybe' look.

Next morning she awoke, Alan still sleeping, dressed and fed Paul and set him in the play-room with a new book with illustrations by Ardizzone.

The doctor returned at the time he had stated, and had made arrangements for Alan's transfer to the home. He found him awake, but looking very shaken and pale. 'You can't help yourself much,' he said, 'and it would be a burden on Emma. They'll look after you well.'

She had already packed his case. He seemed not unwilling to go; he had remembered some of the events of the previous night.

'They'll try to get him off the bottle,' the doctor whispered to Emma, 'which you can't do.'

He helped Alan, who was feeble, downstairs and into the car.

'Be good, darling,' Emma said. 'I shall be in to see you.'

When they had gone she went up to Paul and told him Papa would be away for a little while.

'Is Papa dead?' he asked. He had learned about Stephen.

'No, more or less tired.'

'Will you take me to the park?'

'Of course I will.'

'When's Nanny coming?'

'Tomorrow.'

Emma was terrified by the idea that Nanny might leave her. She had come to depend on the old woman not only for Paul, but for herself.

On the following day, when Mrs Stewart brought in the post, there was a card for her. Emma prayed that the woman had not read it.

SO YOU'VE MARRIED A SOUSE THIS TIME HA HA NOT A GOOD PICKER ARE YOU? WONDER WHAT GIDDY MUMMY THINKS OF IT ALL.

She tore it up and set fire to it in an ashtray.

Chapter Nine

SHE was asked not to go to see him for three days, in order to let him settle down. The doctor said he had had a total collapse. On the second day, however, a letter arrived, in a shaky handwriting.

Darling, I hope you're all right. I am so far as can be expected. When you come tomorrow will you bring me *Stalky and Co.*, some sweets that I can suck, fifty cigarettes and something to drink! I am so thirsty all the time. In haste, all love.

She collected all that he had asked for, including a bottle of lemon squash, the only soft drink that he took, when he took it at all. She found him in an armchair, in pyjamas and dressing-gown, with a rug across his knees. He looked white and curiously youthful. He thanked her for the book, the cigarettes and the fruit drops, but when he saw the bottle he exploded. 'I didn't mean that! Can't you bring me a mouthful of whisky, in a medicine-bottle, so that I don't get found out?'

'I don't think I dare,' she said. 'It's against the rules. But I will ask Donald.'

'I drink that cat's pee all day. You've brought coals to Newcastle. Anyway, do get in touch with Donald and tell him I'm going mad. They dope me half the time.'

'I'll do my best, but I'd better not make promises.'

The room was big and bright, looking over the forecourt on to the main road. It was well appointed, with wash-basin in an alcove and a large wardrobe. 'But how are you, my girl? You didn't tell me. And how's Paul? And Kim?'

'He's fine. I take him out in the park. There was just enough snow for him to play in yesterday. Kim's having fun in it, too. Nanny's back again, thank God. She really is a wonderful old thing.'

'And Mrs Stewart?'

'All right.'

She had told them both that Mr Priest had had a breakdown, owing to hard work, but did not think that either of them believed it. Not that Nanny gave the faintest sign of disbelief, but Mrs Stewart seemed to look askance.

A nurse came in. 'This is Sister Forbes. Sister, my wife.'

'How nice for you to have a visitor, Mr Priest dear. It's time for your tea. Will your wife have a cup?'

'Thank you,' Emma said.

Sister Forbes had a sailor's roll and protuberant green eyes. 'We're doing nicely, Mrs Priest. Mr Priest was in bed all of yesterday.'

'All due to your care, I'm sure,' Emma said.

'Aren't you lovely! I do my best, but he's not an easy patient. Are you, dear?' she added to Alan.

'I do my best,' he replied, 'but I'm so restless.'

'Well, we can't have you running about just yet. All in good time.'

Tea arrived. It was excellent – cucumber sandwiches, bridge rolls with egg, and a home-made spongecake. Emma was delighted to see that Alan ate heartily. 'I'm always hungry here,' he said.

'Shall I bring Paul next time?'

'No, I don't think so. He's young to be subjected to such places. But I'd like to see Kim. You don't mind dogs?' he asked Sister Forbes, when she returned for the tray.

'Not a bit, if they're quiet. Well, Mr Priest dear, you've made a good tea. That will set you up.'

'Who made the cake?'

'Matron. She likes everything to be nice.'

When Emma got home she telephoned the doctor, who told her he thought Alan would have to stay in the home for three weeks at least. She asked him about the whisky.

'Suffering from withdrawal symptoms, is he? Well, they don't practise aversion therapy, so I'll order him a small one only as a nightcap. It will be something for him to look forward to.'

At bed-time, Paul asked her about Papa.

'He's doing well, but I don't think he'll be home for a few weeks.'

'Oh, good,' Paul said, but whether he was referring to the first or second part of her sentence she did not know.

When she returned to the home, she found that Alan was being allowed his nightcap – 'So small, it's a joke,' he said.

'You're looking better, darling.'

'Am I?' he queried. 'I don't know that I feel it. Look at all these flowers. The news has got round to the club, somehow. Sister must think I'm a bloody film star.'

Emma herself had brought him an azalea, hoping it would last. But the room was already embowered with flowers. 'Did you ever see anything like it?' Sister asked.

'Never,' said Emma. 'But they suit him, don't you think?'

'Oh, you're a one, Mrs Priest dear. We take them all out at night, of course.'

At home, Alan's absence was a blessing to Emma. She had not lost all her fondness for him, and would do for him what she could, but love had died. It was peaceful to have dinner quietly with Nanny, and not expect to hear the sound of his key. She unlocked the downstairs cupboard and put back the key.

Agnes came to dinner and she, too, seemed relieved by the peace of it all.

'You're looking better,' she said to Emma. 'I think this break came just at the right time. Alan was getting too much for you.'

'He was,' said Emma, who had not told her mother of the incident with the gun.

'You'll have to watch him when he gets back. These habits are hard to break. You won't keep alcohol in the house?'

'I must, only locked up. If he has friends in, he'll ask for it.'

'Darling, I wish you had a better life.'

'It has all creature comforts, and it has Paul. I couldn't ask for much more.'

Agnes kissed her. 'I think you're very brave.'

'I have to be, for Alan's sake. I owe him something.'

'Why do you?'

'For marrying him when I wasn't quite sure.'

'I didn't know.'

'Nor did I, till recently.'

'If this ever happens again, you'll have to leave him. John and I would look after you.'

'I couldn't. He relies too much on me. I only hope to God that when he comes back they'll have cured him.'

Agnes looked dubious, but she said nothing.

Next day Miss Plimsoll died. They had heard nothing of it, till a solicitor's letter reached Emma. The old lady had left all her money, nine hundred pounds, to Master Paul Hood, to help with his education and be held in trust for him by his mother, Mrs Emma Priest, *née* Sheldrake. To this bequest had been appended, 'Waste not, want not.'

'So she was not so poor as we thought,' Emma said to Agnes. 'Whoever would have thought that she'd leave all that to Paul?'

'I always thought she was taken by him, so much as it was in her to be taken by anybody.'

When Emma visited her husband again she found him fully dressed, but with the rug still over his knees. She told him her news, and he laughed aloud.

'Who'd have thought it of the old girl? Did she really suppose Paul would be in need of it?'

'I think it's rather nice for him to have something of his own. Oh dear, and by the time I heard about it, it was too late for us to go to the funeral.'

Alan said she had told him so much about Miss Plimsoll that he fancied he had known her. 'Waste not, want not, indeed!'

She asked him how he was.

'I'm getting used to it here. And I promise you, darling, that when I get out I shall never revert to type.'

She took his hand and kissed the palm of it. 'Good,' she said.

'You'd be surprised what my nightcap does for me. I hardly feel I want anything else.'

She had brought him some more fruit drops and a copy of Kipling's *Limits and Renewals*. He asked her next time to bring him some Conrad. '*Nostromo*, if you can find it.'

This would be easy. He had always kept his books in impeccable order, never reading while he was drunk.

'They're going to let me walk in the garden for ten minutes tomorrow, if it isn't snowing.'

'Will you like that?'

'If I'm not too shaky on my feet. My girl, I've made a nice mess of myself and everyone else. I'm sorry.'

'Stop feeling sorry,' she said. 'You're going to be all right now. And I'm not frightened that you'll shoot me.'

He winced. 'I'd never have done it.'

'I know you wouldn't. Forget it.'

He had visitors, Jack Hamer and Mrs Hutchinson, who seemed to feel it was all her fault. 'She brought me some peaches,' he said. 'They reminded me of her bottom.'

Time went by. She banked Paul's money in a number two account. The doctor was pleased with Alan, and said he could be home in about a week. 'That's fine,' said Emma rather forlornly. She had been enjoying her bed to herself. Indeed, she had been enjoying her relative solitude, not having to wait for him to come home or wonder in what state he would be. Sometimes the idea of him getting into bed at her side made her shudder. But she continued to go through all the motions of love. She had long ceased to go to church, but she still prayed. 'O Lord, let me love him again.'

At the end of the three weeks he was allowed to come home, accompanied by the doctor. Emma greeted him in the hall. He said jovially, 'Well, Jeeves, the young master is back!'

'Thank you for all you've done, Donald. Will you stay to dinner?'

'I'm afraid I can't. I've got a couple of late calls to make.'

Alone in the drawing-room with Alan, she watched in trepidation to see what move he might make. But he did not go near the drinks cupboard. He said he would like to see Paul, and they both went upstairs together.

Nanny was with the boy. 'Oh, Mr Priest, it's good to see you home again. A kiss for Papa, Paul.'

'You've been a long time,' Paul said. 'Kim missed you.'

'And you didn't?'

'Yes, I did. But Kim runs too fast for me. Even Mummy can't keep up with him.'

When they had said good-night to Paul, Emma went to

unpack for Alan. She laid a new pair of pyjamas out on the bed.

After dinner they spent a quiet evening listening to the wireless. Nanny was asked once more to sit with them. Alan asked for his solitaire board and became absorbed in that. At ten o'clock he rose and went to the drinks cupboard. 'My nightcap,' he said.

'Be careful.'

'It's only the one. I'm used to it.'

But it was a stiff whisky that he poured for himself. Nevertheless, it was all he did seem to have as the weeks went by. He returned to the office and came in sharp at seven. He looked healthy and alert and there was colour in his cheeks. On Saturdays he took to playing nine holes of golf but, so far as Emma could judge, he did not go near the club-house. He came back to lunch on time. On Sundays he took Paul and Kim for a run in the park. There was no snow there now, and Paul was disappointed. 'You'll see other winters, old man,' Alan said to him.

Soon, Emma was sufficiently emboldened to take up afternoon work, unpaid, with the social services. This gave her the feeling that her life was not wasted, though she was only allowed to do the most undemanding jobs, such as manning the telephone. So things continued until, one evening in February, Alan came home late, and when he did so was demonstrably drunk. 'I'm sorry, old girl, but there was an office party. Just don't reproach me.'

'Aunt Issie is coming to dinner. Had you forgotten?'

'Yes, but I can cope.' And he ate what Mrs Stewart had set before him and was able to keep up a conversation with Issie. He had a tight grip on himself all that evening.

Issie said she was doing all right. She still had her job. 'Any time you need a bit of help,' Alan said expansively, 'you can come to Emma and me. Don't forget.'

'Thank you, but I don't need help,' said Issie. She eyed him suspiciously, and seemed glad to take her leave. She had heard from Agnes about his breakdown and his spell in the home.

She gave Emma an unaccustomedly warm good-night kiss. 'Good-bye for now, dear, and remember, if I can ever help you, just let me know.'

Emma despaired of ever keeping any secrets.

She noticed that Alan drank nothing more that night, not even his nightcap, and prayed that this had been no more than a solitary lapse. But Nanny, who always had dinner with them, had seen, and so had Mrs Stewart. Emma began to dislike the housekeeper for what she knew.

Chapter Ten

SHE would have forgotten her birthday – because Alan had forgotten – had it not been for a cashmere twin-set and some cultured pearls from Agnes and Winter, and a coral necklace from Issie.

'What's this all about?' Alan demanded.

'My birthday.'

'God, aren't you young? And I forgot. Never mind, I'll make it up to you. But we must celebrate tonight. We'll have some champagne; that's not dangerous.' He had come to regard champagne as a non-alcoholic drink.

He was home early from the office, bringing with him some *pâté de foie gras*, for which Emma had a guilty love, and an aquamarine brooch. She thanked him warmly and put it on. He kissed her and stood for a minute with his arm around her. 'You're very good to me, my girl. My aged wife. I'm going to be very good to you from now on.'

Nanny, who had heard about the birthday that morning, went out to buy Emma a box of handkerchiefs and some chocolates on behalf of Paul. Mrs Stewart gave her some bath-oil, and Emma was touched. They both seemed so fond of her.

'Will you have a birthday cake, Mummy?'

'No, darling, I'm too old for that.'

'I won't be too old when it's my birthday.' It was not a question but a statement.

'Indeed you won't. You shall have a big one, with pink icing and silver balls on it.'

The early part of that year passed peacefully enough. Every Saturday, Emma played nine holes of golf with Alan, and afterwards visited the club-house where he drank tomato juice.

'Still on the wagon, old boy?' asked Hamer.

'Still on it.'

'Sounds hard-going, but I'm with you. Emma's not on it, though, are you, Emma? Can I get you a gin?'

'Nothing more for me, please. We mustn't be late for lunch.'

'You must have your household in good order,' said Mrs Hamer.

'It has to be, for Paul's routine and Nanny's.'

'You're a lucky girl. I expect Alan thinks so.'

'I do my best to make her lucky,' he said. 'She's worth it.'

Emma flushed. He was free with his compliments these days.

It was not until Easter that the cracks began to show. Twice he came in late and not sober, though he did not drink again that evening. Emma watched him with an anxious heart, and she telephoned the doctor.

'Donald, I'm afraid Alan's beginning again.'

'That's bad news. Keep him off it as far as you can. I'll be in for a routine check on him anyway.'

But Alan would not permit routine checks. 'I'm quite all right, and you can tell Donald so.'

He refused to have his blood-pressure taken. 'My BP's OK. There's nothing for you to worry about. I'm fine.'

The doctor tried to insist, but Alan would not take off his coat. 'I go to the links every Saturday, and I've trained Emma so well that she has nearly beaten me. What more proof do you want?'

The doctor usually saw him in Emma's presence, but on this occasion he asked her to leave them.

When she had gone, he said to Alan, 'Drinking again?'

'Just a spot. Nothing to bother about.'

'I do bother. Let me feel your pulse.'

To this he submitted. 'Anything wrong with that?'

'It's low. I wish you'd let me take your BP.'

'Well, I won't. So you can put that in your pipe and smoke it.'

'I'll have to cease attending you if you go on this way.'

Alan was alarmed by this. 'Come, Donald, you wouldn't desert me.'

'If I can't treat you, I'll have to. I'm doing no good here.'

'Oh, all right. But it's quite unnecessary.'

Afterwards, the doctor warned Emma. 'Let me know if he gets any worse.'

She said she would at once and went back to Alan low-spirited. He asked if the doctor had said anything else to her but she replied that he hadn't. 'Old fusspot,' he grumbled. 'He doesn't want to let me out of his clutches. I'm a paying proposition.'

'You know that's not fair.'

'How do I know what's fair or not? I can only look at the facts.'

On the following night the whisky-bottle appeared on the table by his chair again. He looked at Emma defiantly, waiting for what she would say.

'Oh, darling, no! You don't want to find yourself back in that home.'

'I'm never going to that home again. I can look after my-self.'

'But you upset me! Doesn't that matter?'

'No need to be upset. I know how much I can take.'

He was making love to her sporadically now, and often without success. This she endured, though it left her ex-hausted and frustrated.

A week later he arrived home early, and came along the passage to Paul's bedroom just as Emma was putting him to bed.

'Hullo, old man! Are you going to say good-night to Papa? Give Papa a kiss.' His words were slurred.

But Paul, as soon as Alan's breath reached him, turned his head away.

'What's that for?'

'You smell,' the child muttered.

'Well, you little beast!'

'Don't be angry with him,' Emma said. 'He doesn't know what he's saying. Say you're sorry, Paul.' But Paul said noth-ing.

'I know where I'm not wanted,' said Alan, 'and you're spoiling the kid.' He turned and left the room, banging into the doorpost as he did so. Emma found him in his accustomed chair.

'He was crying,' she said.

'So I should think. Talking to me like that!'

'He's only a little boy.'

'Too grown-up for his own good. I say you spoil him.'

'And I say I don't.'

He said no more, but poured himself a drink. He did not speak again until Mrs Stewart announced that dinner was ready.

'What are we eating?'

'A nice roast leg of lamb,' said the housekeeper, with the air of one humouring a child. She had seen his condition.

'Oh, well, that's all right. I'm not very hungry, though.'

Next morning, when Emma went into the play-room, she saw that Paul had spelled out MR BEAST in his bricks. She dispersed them hastily. 'You mustn't write that.'

'Papa called me a beast.'

'He didn't mean it. It's only his way. He was sad because you wouldn't kiss him good-night.'

'But he smelt,' said Paul obdurately.

She scolded him no further, but left him to Nanny, who had just returned from Cambridge. 'It's a lovely morning. Get him out early.'

'I want to read books.'

'Plenty of time for that,' Nanny said. 'You can read when we come in.'

As a peace-offering, Alan brought him an *Alice in Wonderland*, which Paul was too young to read all by himself. Still, he seemed to like the pictures and this time allowed Alan to kiss him. Emma was glad she had cleared away the bricks.

Alan was getting worse, and did not attempt to touch her in bed. A visit from the doctor had no effect upon him, though he was ordered not to drink at all.

Emma hardly bothered to conceal his state from Nanny and Mrs Stewart. Nanny was afraid of nobody, but Emma saw that the housekeeper was apprehensive. He returned home at all hours, never bothering to eat. He had had something out, he said.

He returned, one cold and blustery night in March, in the middle of dinner and went straight to the drawing-room. Emma and Nanny Harcourt lingered over their meal, afterwards helping Mrs Stewart to clear the table.

They heard a sharp report. Emma went white. 'Don't either of you go into the drawing-room,' she said. 'Nanny, you'd better go up and see whether Paul heard anything. Tell him it was a back-fire.'

She went into the room alone, and when she saw him she thought she would faint. He had put the muzzle of a revolver into his mouth and had pulled the trigger.

She managed to telephone the doctor at once.

'Come quickly,' she said. 'Alan's killed himself.'

He gasped. 'You're sure?'

'When you see what I've seen you'll be sure.'

'I'll phone the police and an ambulance and be along right away.'

She went into the hall where the women were waiting in fear. 'Don't go into the drawing-room on any account. Mr Priest has had an accident. The doctor is coming.'

'I ought to be with you, M'm,' said Nanny, and without waiting for permission went into the room. She started back at what she saw, but made no noise. She put her hand over her mouth.

He had left a suicide note, almost indecipherably scribbled, on the table at his side. 'I can't take any more. Sorry. Love, Alan.'

The doctor came, and shortly afterwards the ambulance and the police. Emma was able to tell the latter all she knew, and to hand over the note. When his body was taken away she did faint. They brought her round and made her lie on the sofa. 'Better tell Mrs Stewart,' she said to Nanny. 'She'll be worrying.'

She asked the doctor for a drink, in a voice that was something between tears and a hysterical giggle. 'Shall I fetch your mother?' he said.

'No. Yes. Do you know the number? It's in the red book by the telephone. It will be better for you to break the news. I couldn't.'

He rang Agnes, who said 'Oh, dear God,' and then was silent. He guessed she was in a state of shock. 'Can you come?' he said. 'Emma needs you.'

'Tell her we're both coming.'

The doctor asked Mrs Stewart for a dust-cover to put over the chair in which Alan had died. 'I'll wait here for it. Don't you come in.'

'Is Mr Priest dead?' Her hands were shaking.

'I'm afraid so. Go along now.'

'Yes, sir. At once.'

He stayed with Emma till the Winters came, asking for tea for her which she did not want. She had not yet begun to cry. 'I'll give you something to make you sleep,' he said.

Agnes and Winter came in. Agnes went straight to Emma. 'Oh, my poor darling! You've had too much to bear.'

'Yes,' said Emma. Now she did begin to cry, leaning against her mother as she had as a child. 'Too much.'

'Get her up to bed as soon as she feels like it,' said the doctor, and took his leave.

'But I don't feel like it yet. He'd been getting worse and worse. He couldn't stop it, though at one time he did try.'

Agnes lit a cigarette for her and put it in her mouth. 'Thank you, Mamma. Will you and John stay the night? Nanny' – for Nanny had unobtrusively returned to her – 'will you make up the beds in the spare room?'

Soon she did allow Agnes to take her upstairs and to undress her. She took the pills the doctor had left, and almost at once went to sleep.

Part Three

Chapter One

EMMA could not bear to live in that house. Having ascertained that Nanny and Mrs Stewart would come back with her to London, if she could find a flat large enough to accommodate them all, she put it up for sale. Alan had left her prosperous, and had bequeathed three thousand pounds to Paul.

With Agnes's help, she found a ten-room apartment in a mansion off the Cromwell Road, no way from the junction with Earl's Court Road. There was an ample sitting-room and bedroom for Mrs Stewart, a large bedroom for Nanny and Paul, a spare room which would do for Paul's play-room.

'I hope it will suit you,' she said to Nanny.

'As if I would ever leave you and Paul, M'm.'

The move took some time. There were redecorations to do. The previous tenant had attempted to bring down the high ceilings by painting them ox-blood red and bottle green. Emma had them repainted in light blue (for Paul) and cream.

Paul was the only one to resent the move. He missed the garden, and he knew Kim would miss it more.

He took his revenge by climbing on to the lavatory seat in the flat and hurling out what objects of glass and china he could find. Most of their wedding-presents went that way into the well, and Emma had to apologise to the porter.

'Your loss, not mine, Ma'am,' he said stoically, and swept up the mess.

Emma understood Paul. Taking him on her knee she said, 'Look, love, we know you miss the garden. But we're only a bus ride from the Zoo here, and you can see things far more exciting than the deer.' In fact, the number 74 bus took them to the gates. So, on the Sundays that were not Mrs Stewart's day off, to the Zoo they went, Emma and Nanny and Paul. But the child was not altogether comforted, though he enjoyed his trips to Holland Park and to the wilderness of Brompton Cemetery, which he did not recognise for what it was. On Saturdays Emma took him on the same bus, though in the opposite direction, to Wimbledon Common, where there were trees he could pretend to climb. All in all, they settled in fairly well.

Emma had got a good price for the house and garden and was glad to be rid of both.

She had told Paul that his stepfather had had an accident with a gun and was dead. This he took with some equanimity, and the next day Nanny found he had spelled out in his bricks, BEAST IS DED. This she hastily erased and gave him a scolding a good deal worse than his mother would have done. For at least an hour he was cowed.

Emma was glad to be back in London. She opened an account at Harrods, bought herself another four-poster bed and some clothes. She liked being nearer Agnes, to whom she was becoming more attached, though she shared no private thoughts with her.

These mostly hinged on her sexual deprivation. As time went by, so it got worse with her. She prayed for it to pass her by, but she was trapped in the poorhouse of her flesh. She did not seek self-gratification. She remembered her mother's horror when, at the age of nine, she had confessed to the habit. 'You will either go blind or go mad!' Though she did not believe a word of this, it now aroused in her an acute sense of guilt. She wished she had been made differently, demanding little, like Agnes, and could go to bed each night without the ache and the loneliness. Yet she was determined not to marry again. 'I should feel like Bluebeard,' she told Agnes when the subject cropped up. No, she must be quiet and placid.

But not so easy. Her days were taken up with Paul, for whom she had found a new nursery school, and she took him there for the mornings. When he was older he could go to a school in Queen's Gate for boys between five and eight. Nanny would have made the two morning trips but Emma would not let her. She was getting too old. However, she let Nanny take him to Holland Park, partly in his push-chair and partly walking. Mrs Stewart had settled down in her ample quarters and she found the shopping easier.

At the back of the flats were private gardens, where Emma could exercise Kim, when he was not racing around with Nanny and Paul in Holland Park.

Paul was settling down into his new school where, under an admirable mistress called Miss Burroughs, he was continuing with his reading and his tables. He was happy, though longing to go on to higher things. He remained equable, sweet-tempered and slow to anger. Emma knew she was lucky in him.

She held a belated house-warming in the flat, to which she invited all her old friends, Agnes and Winter, and suggested that for old times' sake her mother should make a bread pudding. But this, alas, was eaten more out of politeness than enthusiasm. Dicky brought his guitar – he had progressed from the ukulele – and they danced for a while to the wireless. But the old days had gone, and she knew it.

Sylvia was now married to a pleasant-faced man called Ian Ross, who reminded Emma of Stephen. Noel had been down from Oxford for the event, and had called to see Paul. 'My nephew,' he said proudly. He was doing well and would soon be sitting for his Schools. The elder Hoods took to seeing Emma again regularly, and made much of her, though her marriage to Alan was never mentioned. She had taken up embroidering in wool on jerseys and cardigans, and could do so without a pattern, as if she were painting. Life on the surface went equably for her.

Paul was now getting on for five, and growing more like Stephen, she thought, with every day. Nanny was devoted to him and to Emma. He was now at school morning and after-noon, and there was nothing much for her to do but look after his clothes and Emma's. She was getting old but was still active, taking him to Holland Park and the Zoo in Emma's stead.

Rumours had reached England, through a sizeable trickle of refugees, of Hitler's treatment of the Jews, which was, to say the least of it, disquieting. Emma had made two Jewish friends, living on the floor above her, and was aware of their

anxiety. 'We don't feel really safe,' they said, 'even here.'
Though not themselves refugees, they had relations in Berlin.
Emma, becoming a shade more political, was anxious for
them. They were well-to-do city merchants, who kept open
house for all the people they liked, whether Jew or Gentile.
They were called Levy.

Through them she met a pleasant boy of twenty-one who
was much taken with her. He was a Scotsman and his name,
like her housekeeper's, was Stewart. He had only recently left
the university, where he had known Noel slightly. He asked if
he might call on her once a week on his way to the Levys, and
she saw no harm in this. Gradually they became intimate and
she told him the miserable story of her second marriage. For
some reason he invited confidences and got them.

She was pleased to talk; there was no one else whom she
could talk to so easily. They sat before the small coal fire –
there was central heating – and she treated him as if she knew
him better than she did. He was of middling height with dark
curling hair and dark eyes. He looked older than his years. She
believed that he had never had a woman.

'My God, you have had a rough time,' he said. 'I think
you've been marvellous.'

'Not that, but I had to hold things together for Paul's sake.'

One evening, the whole of which he was spending with her
while the Levys were on holiday, he told her that he loved her.

'Don't be absurd, Mark!' she said, aghast. 'I'm much older
than you are.'

'Not so very much. And it's true, what I say. You don't
have to reciprocate, but just let me love you. That's all.'

'No, I can't.'

'You can't stop me.'

'I can stop seeing you.'

'You wouldn't be so cruel.'

'You don't know how cruel I can be.'

'No, and I don't even suspect it.'

When she was wearing a long skirt, which she often did in
the evenings, he would sit at her feet, like a troubadour (she
thought) and pour out to her his ambitions and his hopes. He
meant to be a writer, he said, whatever happened. He showed

her two poems (bad) and two short stories which she thought rather good. He hoped to get a grant of some kind to enable him to carry on. 'But you could work *and* write,' Emma said. 'Trollope did, and so did Fielding. And Shakespeare must have worked as an actor, besides writing plays.'

'Ah, but I'm not them, my dear,' he said rather quaintly, 'and I haven't their staying power.'

One night he came in with *Life* magazine. He showed her a photograph of an elderly Jew wearing only his drawers and a placard, led through the Berlin streets by Stormtroopers. Mark was grinning. 'Isn't he exactly like Tom Levy, poor devil?'

'How can you laugh!' She tore out the page, crumpled it and threw it on the fire. 'You didn't intend to show that to Tom?'

'I didn't mean to laugh. That is, I know it's not funny. No, I didn't mean to show it to him. I was only going to lend them the magazine. They like to have it.'

'With that in it?'

'I suppose so. I didn't think. Sorry.'

She told him he had better be. 'Tom and Pearl are so good and kind.'

'Always putting my big foot in it.'

'Well, try not to.' But she thought the less of him.

However, she asked him to dinner one night and he accepted eagerly. Mrs Stewart seemed suspicious of her namesake and gave them a meal less enthusiastically than was her wont. They had some wine, however, and all went well. Nanny would not join them. 'I don't care to, when you have visitors, M'm,' she said. 'I'd much rather not. I'll have mine with Florence.' (This was Mrs Stewart.) She did not care for 'that boy', as she called him privately, and was displeased that he paid so little attention to Paul, who was often in his dressing-gown and slippers when Mark came in the early evening. These feelings she managed, without words, to convey to Emma.

Emma, though she felt she could see right through Mark and his blandishments, could not help being attracted to him. He was a life-giver. She always behaved as though she were ten years his senior, sometimes taking him to a theatre or a concert. He repaid her with adoration. Soon he had taken her advice to write *and* work, and had found a part-time job in a bookshop. 'Now you'll be pleased with me,' he said, 'and I shall feel less of a scrounger.' He bought her flowers, and seemed to take more interest in Paul, who was now accepted, a full year early, for the pre-preparatory school in Queen's Gate.

He was reading fluently now and knew all his tables. He had a phenomenal memory. She took him for an interview with the headmaster, who tested him first with a children's book and then with an adult novel. He heard his eight- and twelve-times table. 'Well, Mrs Priest,' he said, 'he's far advanced. I think we can take him in the autumn term.'

When they were outside in the street, she hugged him. 'Clever boy. Soon you'll be learning Latin and French! Your daddy would have been proud of you.' She took him to church on Sundays but let him come out before the sermon. 'But I wouldn't mind staying,' he said.

'No, enough is enough.'

Mark, who had learned of her faith, teased her gently about it. 'And you a big girl. Can you take the Thirty-Nine Articles?'

'Not all thirty-nine of them, perhaps. And I leave out bits of the Creed.'

'You must take me one Sunday.'

'A heathen like you? Not on your life. You'd come to mock and remain to mock.'

'I swear I wouldn't. You might even convert me. I'd do anything for you.' But she did not take him to church with her.

She took him to dinner with Agnes and Winter, and at once sensed that her mother did not care for him. 'I should be careful of that young man if I were you,' her mother said on the telephone next day. 'I fancy he's after what he can get. And he ought to do some proper work. I admit he has his attractions.'

'There's nothing for me to be careful about,' said Emma, 'and I'm not fifteen.'

'I could wish you were, again.'

One day Mark brought a friend along to meet Emma. His name was Jim Clegg, and he was her own age. 'Jim looks after me like a mother hen,' he said.

The relationship between the two young men was puzzling.

They did not seem especially close. Jim treated Mark like a schoolboy, while admiring his literary gifts. It was a great day when Mark sold a short story to *Nash's Magazine*, and Emma gave them both champagne to celebrate. 'Now you're truly launched,' she said.

'He's a clever old thing, isn't he?' said Jim lazily. He himself was on a graduate course at Imperial College. 'We'll see him among the bestsellers yet.'

For this, Mark received a fee of twenty-five pounds and he took Emma out to dinner on the strength of it. It was a pleasure to him to play host. They went to a restaurant in Soho, one with check tablecloths and red candles. 'You have some whitebait,' he said. 'You know you love them.'

Over the coffee, he became sentimental. The hour and the glow became him. 'You know, my life has completely changed since I met you. I never met anyone so calm and collected and you've been through the mill – I know.'

'All that's past and forgotten,' she said.

'I can't forget. And I want you to know that I admire you more than anyone I've ever met.'

He gave a mock flinch, as if she had made to strike him.

'Don't be angry with me. You know one can't help these things.' He took her hand and kissed it. 'That's how I feel about you.'

'Don't,' she said.

'But you don't altogether hate me, do you? Even if I am a bit pushing?'

'You know very well I don't. But I don't like it when you try to make love to me.'

'I wish I was ten years older! Then you'd listen.'

'I shouldn't. I only want friendship.'

'But you must get lonely, sometimes?'

This seemed to her to be taking advantage of her confidences, which, however, had never included her most private thoughts.

'I am quite all right. Paul's all I need.'

'But some day, you'll need something else, won't you? I adore you. Jim adores you, too. Shall we have another bottle?' He gestured to the waiter.

She refused. She had had enough, and so had he. At last they went out into the glare of Soho, and he took her arm. She hailed a taxi. 'At least you'll let me pay for that.' But he would not. His money was lasting out. In the taxi, under the crossing lights of passing traffic, he kissed her. She did not respond, but she did not repulse him, either. It seemed to her a milestone for them both, and when she was home she bitterly regretted it. She was not in the least in love with him and it seemed to her that she had given him a licence to go farther in their relationship.

She saw little of the Levys these days, though she found them both cordial when they met in the hall by the lift. Mark visited them, but less often, preferring to stay with Emma until dinner was ready. He had had no luck yet with further stories, but had started a novel. It appeared to be all about undergraduates and their souls. Emma sighed with exasperation.

Chapter Two

THEY had a letter from Eric Flowers. He was in hospital, undergoing tests. 'It is very boring in here, so if you – either of you – could spare an hour I should be grateful. I have had to let the bungalow go to rot, for all I care. My Cochran girl-friend has deserted me. I don't get much of what I want out of life.'

'Poor old thing,' said Agnes. 'He was always trying to be so young, and it didn't work. We might go down on Sunday.'

They did so. They found him in a private room, lying in bed, and looking yellow. They brought him flowers and some chocolates. Dapperness had deserted him, and his small moustache had been shaved off. 'When I think of the old days,' he said, 'and both of you doing the Charleston on my veranda, I could weep.'

'You were very kind to us,' said Emma. 'I shan't forget my honeymoon.'

He rose on his elbow, fumbled in his locker, asked them for a cigarette and a light. 'I'm allowed these privileges in here.'

He wanted to know about the latest shows, the latest films. 'Keep me up to date. I have to be, or I'd go crazy.'

On their way out, they spoke to the ward sister about him.

'Mr Flowers is very ill, I'm afraid,' she said, 'but we're still waiting for the results of his tests.'

'Poor dear, he hasn't got much out of life,' said Agnes as they got into her car. 'And he did like to be so cheerful. I'm so sorry for him. He was always so kind.'

'I used to love him in his little blue blazer with the brass buttons and his white ducks. I wonder why he never married?'

'I expect because the kind of girls he liked didn't care for him. They were always in the chorus and very young, you know.'

But in the autumn they had news of him from a friend. He

had terminal cancer, inoperable. He would like to see them, as he had something to tell them.

So they drove again to the hospital. He was lying on his back, looking very ill. He did not smile. He thanked them for the flowers and magazines they had brought, and asked them to sit down on either side of the bed. For a while he did not speak. Then he said, with an effort, 'I've had something on my mind and I haven't long to go. I used to write you beastly postcards,' he said to Emma. 'I must have been mad. But it seemed to me that you had everything and I had nothing. I'm sorry. I'd give my eyes not to have done it.'

They, too, for a moment, were shocked into speechlessness. Then Emma said, 'It doesn't matter now.' Yet he had sent her the first card just before she went for her honeymoon in his bungalow. 'You mustn't think about it any more.'

'And I can't make it up to you. I've left you something in my will.'

'Don't worry, don't fret,' said Agnes. 'Anyway, it's all over now and we've forgotten it.' But she had lost colour.

'When I can sit up,' Flowers said with a ghastly smile, 'I'll read your magazines.'

Emma put a hand over his. 'We'll come again.'

He said, 'Don't. I'd rather you didn't. It only reminds me. Anyway, as I said, I haven't long to go.' He withdrew his hand from Emma's.

On their way home, Agnes said, 'Curse him.'

'Mamma, don't. He's sufficiently cursed already.'

'When I think of the distress it caused you. . . .'

'Oh, I'm tough. I survived. The police were so sure it was a woman.'

'Women are usually associated with poison-pen letters.'

'And he's truly sorry.'

'So he ought to be.'

'You're hard,' Emma said.

'I can't help being. I was thinking of you.'

A fortnight later, they heard that he was dead.

Paul was admitted to the pre-preparatory school. He wore a grey coat and grey trousers, and blue and grey socks and cap. He looked very important.

'My big boy,' said Emma. 'Do well.'

'I'll try,' said Paul. 'But the boys will be much bigger than me.'

At the end of term, he was top of the junior class and about to be moved upwards.

'He's a wonderful little boy,' said the headmaster. 'Do you want him to do boxing next term?'

'But the odds are bound to be against him. I should like him to wait for a while.'

'It's whatever you wish, Mrs Priest.'

'I should always defer to your judgement.'

'Then let us wait awhile for the boxing. If a boy should have a weak chest, I should advise against it. Not that they can hit one another so hard at that stage.'

'Paul's chest seems all right, up to now,' Emma said.

But she spoke almost too soon. That term Paul had a bout of bronchitis and was away from school for a fortnight. 'That will mean they'll all catch up with me,' he fretted.

'Don't you bother about that. All we want is for you to get quite well.'

'I will get well,' said Paul, and turned to a book.

The doctor was pleased with him. Paul responded to treatment well, and was good about taking medicine. He soon went back to school.

Mark was Emma's constant visitor – Mark, and sometimes Jim Clegg. She allowed both young men to kiss her lightly now, on arrival and departure. Emma had had her piano brought out of storage, and she practised for half an hour every day, though she was very rusty. Mark, seeing it, asked if he could play it. She discovered that he played and sang well, sang in a light tenor voice.

> 'In Scarlet Town, where I was born,
> There was a fair maid dwelling,
> Made every youth cry well-a-day,
> Her name was Barbara Allan.'

Paul wandered in, asking for a glass of water. 'I heard the music,' he said. Nanny Harcourt was on leave and Mrs Stewart off for the day. 'Shall I go on?' Mark asked.

'Please,' said Emma, 'it will be a treat for Paul.' She took him on her knee.

> 'Then slowly, slowly, came she up,
> And slowly came she by him,
> And all she said when there she came,
> "Young man, I think you're dying."'

Mark continued to the end. When he had done, Paul said 'Thank you' politely, and slipped from Emma's knee. He seemed to have forgotten all about the glass of water, but she gave it him. 'Ready for bed, now?'

He said he was. She saw him back into it, then returned to Mark. 'That was beautiful,' she said. 'I couldn't have guessed that you'd be half as good. Do go on.' So he played and sang to her for another hour.

Emma began having small after-dinner parties again – the Levys, Mark, Jim Clegg and sometimes Sylvia and Ian Ross. Often Mark would sing to them, and Nanny was called in to listen. She came with reluctance. Really she was happier listening to the wireless with Mrs Stewart. She now took Paul to school and fetched him each day. The boys all waited on the steps for parents to fetch them, and on those days when Emma went she thought it looked like a slave-market. You expected one of the fathers to point with an umbrella and say, 'I'll have that one.' She was now more content than she had been for a long time, though the call of her body still irked her. She wished she had been like her mother, satisfied with so little. Once or twice she dreamed of her father, whom she had almost forgotten.

One night early in November, Mark came to her in a state of distress, hardly able to tell her what was the matter. At last he managed it. Jim had been arrested in the lavatory at Leicester Square, for indecent behaviour.

She was so shocked that she did not watch her words, and her vague suspicions came to the surface. 'And are you the same?' she burst out.

'No,' he said. He seemed on the verge of tears.

'But you knew what he was?'

'It didn't seem any of my business. We were at school together.'

'Because if you were—'

'I'd have shown you what I was, if you'd given me half the chance.' He seemed furious.

'I'm sorry, so sorry.'

'For what? For Jim, or for what you said?'

'For both. Is he out on bail?'

'Yes.'

'Who stood bail for him?'

'I did.'

'But if he skipped how would you afford it?'

'He won't.'

Emma asked what the sum was, and said she would pay it in case of necessity. She tried to calm him down and thought she had succeeded, when he took and kissed her violently, thrusting his tongue between her lips. 'Don't,' she said.

'I'll show you.' But he returned to his place on the divan. Then he did burst into tears, and she was at a loss to know how to console him. She lent him her handkerchief and fetched him a drink. He looked ridiculously young. The kiss had excited her, though she dared not show this. She watched in silence while he wiped his eyes and drank the brandy.

'I couldn't help it,' he said.

Next day, Jim Clegg appeared in court and was fined. He did not come to her parties again, and no one asked any questions.

Then, one night about two weeks later, Mark called on her again. He was in a state of excitement. He said, 'I want to make love to you. You're driving me mad.'

'Don't be silly,' she replied. 'You know you mustn't be.'

Nanny was on leave and Mrs Stewart having her day off.

But he pushed her on to the divan and began to unzip her dress. He was unexpectedly strong. 'Please,' he said. That night she let him take her. She was sick and ashamed, but the relief was wonderful. She dressed again, him watching her. 'You must never do that any more.'

'You know you liked it,' said Mark.

171

From that night on they were lovers. He took the precautions, or so she thought. 'Do you love me?' he asked her.

'A little. But you're so young.'

'Not quite three years younger than you are. And I don't want to hear any more about that.'

They went twice a week to Mark's shabby but neat bed-sitting room in Earl's Court. They were frightened lest Nanny and Mrs Stewart should find out about them. Mark seemed to Emma to be growing up; he was, she found, not quite inexperienced, and now that he had her he tended to take the upper hand. She felt invigorated and, as time went on, less troubled by thoughts of guilt. She was not in love with Mark, but she was grateful for him. Then, at the beginning of the New Year, she began to fear that she might be pregnant.

She wasted no time. She went to a new doctor, a stranger to her, and consulted him. He took a sample of her urine and said he would telephone her in a day or two's time. When he did so he said, 'Yes, Mrs Priest, you're going to have a baby. My congratulations.' He told her of a clinic where she could go for supervision. He said she should smoke less and drink very little.

She was frantic. It seemed to her that she must tell Mark at once, though she was determined not to marry him. He at once proposed to her. 'I haven't much money, but we can get along between us.' He seemed proud at the prospect of parenthood. 'I'm sorry,' Emma said, 'but I shall never marry again.'

'That's crazy. I'd marry you tomorrow.'

'No.'

'Then what will the child be called?'

'By my maiden name, Sheldrake.'

'Oh, do have some sense! It's my child, too.'

'Marrying three times, at my age, looks like Messalina. Besides, I should want a marriage to last, and this one wouldn't.'

Try as he might, he could not budge her. She went to confess to her mother.

Agnes was aghast. 'You know whose it is?'

'Don't insult me, Mamma.'

'And won't he marry you?'

'He wants to, but I won't. I'm never going to marry again.'

'Where are you going to have it?'

'In a hospital. The doctor will arrange it.'

'Look here, darling, do you mind if I tell John? Three heads may be better than two.'

She did not mind. She told her story, and of her refusal to remarry, and he listened in grave silence.

'I must say, Emma, that you're being very foolhardy. How are you going to look after it?'

'I'm perfectly capable, and perhaps Nanny will stay.'

'You know we'll do all we possibly can for you. How long is it?'

'Only about five weeks.'

'Perhaps you could go to another doctor,' Agnes said, 'and see whether anything could still be done.'

'An abortion? No. That would be murder.' Emma was adamant. She still felt some guilt over her relations with Mark, and was not going to add to it by a crime. It was a crime in her eyes.

'But if you were found unfit to have another—'

'I'm perfectly fit, Mamma. I've never felt better.'

'Have you thought about Paul? He'll ask questions.'

'He might like a brother or sister. I shall tell him when the time's nearer.'

Then Agnes rose and hugged and kissed her. Emma felt herself trembling. Confession had been more of a strain than she thought. She realised that she had been living through a nightmare.

She lit a cigarette. The habit was harder than she had thought to break. She warmed more towards Winter, who was being so kind, even if so helpless. In the bright, rich room she felt stronger than he.

She told Nanny Harcourt the next day, and sensed the shock she had given. But Nanny still sat quietly, her hands folded in her lap. 'And will you be marrying again, M'm?'

'No. I'm determined not to.'

'But to give the baby a name—'

'Not even for that. Mark is the father, by the way.'

'That boy!'

'Not such a boy. He asked me to marry him, though.'

'Surely it's the best thing you can do, M'm?'

'It may be, but I'm not doing it. You'll stand by me, Nanny, won't you?'

'I'll do my best. But I'm too old for a new baby.'

'You'll never be too old, Nanny dear. I'm sorry if this has upset you.'

'We must do everything for the best,' Nanny said, but not helpfully.

Chapter Three

MARK sulked, Emma thought, like a débutante at a ball. He had been so determined to marry her. After a quarrelsome three weeks, he took action, leaving his Earl's Court bed-sitter and moving into Jim Clegg's flat in Kensington. This seemed to confirm all Emma's fitful suspicions.

She did not conceal her condition from anyone. The one most shocked was Mrs Stewart, who found that she had to keep house for a sick brother. Emma parted from her with regret, but advertised for someone else and soon found her, though the woman was far more expensive. She was a Mrs Harper, and she loved dogs. Perhaps Kim would be fed better than anyone else.

Only one person had received her decision not to marry with sang-froid. This was Sylvia Ross, who said, 'Well, sweetie, it's your own business.' Sylvia was now pregnant herself, and even more tolerant than usual. 'Mind you,' she said, 'Mark's a nice enough boy.' The word fell like lead on Emma's ears. A boy was what he was. The elder Hoods tried to put pressure upon her, but found her intractable. 'But, Emma, you'll be storing up so much trouble for yourself and Paul,' Mrs Hood said. 'You must think for you both.'

Agnes and Winter were deeply distressed. It was not so much her pregnancy that worried them, but her rooted decision not to marry. The baby, Agnes said, would be bound to carry a stigma. 'What a disgusting phrase,' said Emma.

In the meantime, there was much for them to worry about in the world outside. In March, Hitler occupied the Rhineland. 'The only thing to do would have been to stop him now,' Emma said. 'We don't know what he'll want next.'

Alan's political lessons were all that was left to her.

One night Jim Clegg called, alone, at her flat. He stopped at the threshold when she opened the door. 'You know all about me. Are you going to let me in?'

Emma said that of course she was. She took him to the drawing-room where she gave him a drink. He looked, she thought, wholly masculine – more so than Mark, who would have made a pretty girl.

'I don't exactly come as an emissary,' Jim said, 'because Mark doesn't know I'm coming at all.'

'And you know all about me,' said Emma. 'What have you come to say?'

'To plead with you to marry Mark. He's mad about you and about his coming child. He always wanted to be a father.'

'Well, that's all he will be, and no more.' Emma was obdurate. She sipped her own drink and lit a cigarette. 'I've told him; I shall never marry again.'

'You realise that it's fine that he should want to marry you? Many men in his position would be running for their life.'

His tone was not conciliatory, but hostile.

'He can run for it, for all I care. We had a happy time together and that's all.'

She added, 'Tell him that I should always be glad to take it up again. Though that's all.'

'You are tough.'

'I have to be.'

'But why?' Jim sounded bewildered.

'Because I've made up my mind.'

He paused. Then he said, 'You're not suspicious of him and me? Because there's no need. He's not made that way.'

'And what may that be?'

'Blighted, of course,' he said, but he grinned. She did not know how to deal with him.

'What sort of a marriage would it be?' Emma asked.

'A kind of *mariage blanc*, if you wanted it that way. He doesn't. But a trip to the registry office doesn't take much time.' He would see to the arrangements, Jim added.

'And yourself as best man?' She was now hostile, too.

'You don't need a best man at a registry office.'

'I've had enough of marriage. My best was when we were so

176

poor we had to have the bath under the kitchen table, and my mother helped to keep us.'

'No, I didn't know that. You were never for taking me into your confidence, you know.'

'Well, it was so. And my next marriage ended in tragedy, if you can call a drunken man putting a bullet into his head a tragedy.'

'I can. And I know you can.'

'Go and tell Mark that I will not marry him, but that he shall have access to the child as soon as it's born.'

Jim stood up. 'And that's your last word?'

'My last.'

'I pity you. Though I suppose you don't want my pity.'

'Yes, I shall need pity, I know. Thank you, Jim.'

He stared at her. She now knew what it was like to be stared at, but not to be admired. She wondered whether he had even glimpsed what Mark had seen in her. When he took his leave he gently kissed her cheek. 'Don't think too badly of me. But I had to try.'

'I'm sorry it was of no use.'

The door closed behind him.

'Dinner's ready,' said Mrs Harper. She was a good plain cook, not an elaborate one, like Mrs Stewart. Emma and Nanny ate rabbit pie and baked apples.

She concealed her condition from none of her friends. Sylvia, though unshockable, could not understand Emma's reluctance to marry, even if it were for a third time.

'Messalina,' Emma said.

'But, sweetie, that child's got to have a name. What will Paul think, when he's old enough?'

'Paul will think what I tell him to.'

'You can't get it taken away? I believe it can be done.'

'As I told my mother, that's murder. The baby's a living creature already.'

Sylvia did not pursue the subject.

Mark visited Emma once a week, and still pleaded with her, though he made no attempt to make love to her. For her part, her pregnancy had cooled her desires. She tried to live peaceably, took Kim to Holland Park to exercise him, and accepted all invitations. Her worry was what she should tell Paul when the time came. How would he feel, and what would he ask her? Who would be the father? She did not know how she would answer. These questions seemed to resolve themselves satisfactorily; nevertheless she had bad dreams. One of these was that her baby was born dead, and a group of black-robed figures stood by her bedside pestering her with questions. But what does it matter now? she said to them. They replied: It will always matter.

And perhaps it would, whatever she did in her waking hours.

She was being badgered by Agnes and Winter. They had long since refused to take a reserved stance, and brought all their weight to bear upon her. 'If you go on like this, Mamma, I will never come to see you again.'

Agnes was flustered. 'My darling, you don't know what you're saying.'

'Nor do you' said Emma.

'That sounds rude! And you were never rude.'

'I'm sorry if it did. But you and John do worry me so. You must leave me to live my own life.'

'I wouldn't be human if I didn't think you were living it wrong. Darling, you know we want only the best for you.'

'And I'm having the best, believe me.'

'But, Mark, and that poor child—'

'Mark understands me, on the whole. And it won't be a poor child.' It was warm in the drawing-room, and Emma took off her cardigan.

'Are you attending the clinic regularly?'

'Quite regularly. I don't want any harm to come to it.'

'Would you like John and me to adopt it?'

'That's generous of you, but no. I can manage all by myself. And how could you explain it away, anyhow?'

There seemed to be no answer to this.

'I can't think why you slept with Mark if you didn't love him!' Agnes burst out.

'Because I was lonely. I'm sorry now.'

'Oh, my poor girl.'

'Please don't pity me. I don't want to see any friend who does that. I'm strong-willed.'

'I'm afraid you are. Too strong for your own good.'

Emma looked around her at the luxurious hangings, the dark, polished wood of sideboard and bureau. Changing the subject she said, 'Do you remember when we only had three rooms? Those were the days. How we all danced, and had fun!'

'We had to work for it.'

'I know you did, Mamma. But it was fun all the same. And I had Stephen.'

'Well, later on, I had John. But, yes, we did have some good times.'

'We never worried then, about people like Hitler. But I suppose we might have worried about Mussolini.'

'I don't worry about Hitler now,' said Agnes. 'I don't know enough to worry.'

The next night, when they were dining alone, Emma asked Nanny Harcourt why she had never married.

Nanny flushed. 'I don't know. And I was always so taken up with the children. I don't feel I've missed anything.'

'Yet you must have been a pretty girl. Didn't your employer's husband ever have an eye for you?'

'I should have known how to send him packing if he did. Though I was only an under-nurse then.'

'Have some more mousse. Yes, do. You know you never put on any weight.'

'No more do you, M'm.'

'And I wish you'd call me Emma.'

'Oh, I couldn't do that. It wouldn't seem right. I'll carry on in the old way, if it's all the same to you.'

'It's not quite the same to me, but let it go.'

They talked of the coming child. Nanny had carefully preserved most of Paul's layette and was knitting some matinée jackets. Together they bought some new nightgowns: Nanny did not believe in dressing a small baby up every day. 'Plenty of time for frills when they're able to sit up.'

She did most of her knitting in the drawing-room with Emma, tactfully withdrawing whenever Mark came. Emma could tell that he was a favourite of hers, despite the feeling she must harbour that he had sinned. But Nanny, chapel or no chapel, had a tolerant soul.

Of Alan, nothing was ever said. He might never have existed.

Chapter Four

IN MAY, Emma decided that she would learn to drive. She had tried before, with Alan, but she had been too tense and he too impatient for any progress to be made. This time she joined the British School of Motoring, and had her lessons on a dual-control car under the tuition of a middle-aged man with long side-whiskers and a moustache. It seemed that with him she would be equally unsuccessful. Perhaps because she was carrying a child her reflexes were slower than usual, and she was more nervous. She could not yet even steer straight around a corner, and inevitably clashed her gears. 'Easy does it, easy does it,' said the instructor, but it was by no means clear what easy did what. He drove her out to some quiet streets beyond Belsize Park, and there let her do her worst. It was a very bad worst. She had a fear of running over a child, and had only to see one playing with a ball to stamp on her brakes.

'Now, Mrs Priest, what was that for?'

'He might have sent the ball into the road and come running after it.'

'You'll have to get rid of all those fears, you know.'

But she could not. She made sufficient progress to be promoted to the busier streets where at least the threat of children was less.

At last, after a fortnight of this, she was driving down Baker Street in the rush hour when, behind a bus, she simply folded her hands in her lap. 'I can't see what is going to stop me running into that.'

'I can,' said the instructor grimly, and took over. At the end of that terrible hour she plucked up courage and said, 'I'm giving up. I shall never be any better and I know when to stop.'

'Madam,' he said, 'I've never been so glad to hear anyone say anything like that in my life.'

So the driving lessons came to an end and she had recourse to her bicycle. The whole affair had cost her twenty-five pounds.

Agnes teased her, and it was near to jeering. 'Of course you can drive, darling, if only you persist. Everyone is nervous at first. I certainly was.'

'I find that hard to believe. But I shall never stop being. I know that now.'

Paul was disappointed. 'I thought you'd fetch me in a big car, as some of the mummies do, Scrimgeour and Holback. That would have been lovely.'

'I can't drive, old man, and that's that. Some people can and some can't.'

She still wondered how she was to tell him about the baby. She was just beginning to show her pregnancy, and was already in a maternity dress. But, in the event, she never had to tell him.

It was June. The Spanish Civil War had just broken out, and Emma was passionately for the Government. She thought, as many people did, that in the event of a war with Hitler Franco would control the Straits of Gibraltar.

One fine Saturday, Emma and Mark took Paul on the bus to Putney Heath. They sat on the upper deck, as Emma liked to smoke and Paul to look out of a front window. They walked across to the borders of Wimbledon Common and Paul, running ahead of them, made rather pitiful attempts to climb trees. He was not an athletic child. He resisted Mark's proffered assistance in getting to the higher branches. 'Thank you,' he said politely, 'but I'm up far enough.'

It was beautiful weather, mild and blue, and a light wind ruffled the grasses. They walked as far as the Windmill, where Paul had an ice-cream, and then down the slopes to Queensmere. The little boy seemed very happy. He liked Mark, who would still sing to him occasionally, and he loved Emma, to whose hand he clung.

'Getting tired, old boy?' Mark said. 'Perhaps we'd better be getting back. It's a fair way to the bus. I'll give you a piggyback if you like.'

But Paul was too proud. 'I'm not a bit tired,' he said, though he began to lag when they got on to the Heath again and the bus terminus was in sight. 'You can have another ice-cream when we get to it,' Emma said.

'Oh, can I? Thank you, Mummy.'

At last they came to the terminus. They climbed again to the top deck of a 74 bus, which would take them almost to their door. The deck was empty but for themselves, so they all sat in the front seats.

When they were approaching Cromwell Road they went to the head of the stairs, Emma going first, ready to climb down. Just as the bus was slowing up by the request stop, the driver braked violently to avoid some obstruction ahead. Emma, losing her balance, hurtled right down the steps and only saved herself from falling in the road by gripping the central pole.

'Are you all right, Mummy?' Paul cried out. He followed her, Mark after him. They stood on the platform and the conductress came to them.

'That was a nasty one, love. Sure you're OK?'

'I think so,' Emma said. She was white and shaken. 'I've dropped my bag.'

'I'll hold the bus while I pick up your things.' The conductress retrieved a powder-compact, a lipstick, a packet of cigarettes and a few scattered coins. 'That do you?'

'Thank you. You're very kind.'

'I should go home and get a lie-down if I were you.'

She watched them as they crossed the road, the woman between the child and the man, who held both her arms.

When they were back in the flat, Paul said tremulously, 'Mummy, you're as white as snow!'

Emma kissed him. 'It's only because of that silly tumble. I shall be quite all right again soon. Now, you go to Nanny, tell her what has happened and ask her to get you some tea. Can you do all that?'

They heard him calling 'Nanny! Nanny!' as he ran away down the passage.

Mark settled her on the sofa and brought her a stiff drink. 'Are you sure you're going to be all right, darling? What about the kid?'

'The doctor says one mustn't worry too much about falls.

The baby is swimming like a peach in a can protected by the juice. It's a nice image, I think. Give me a cigarette.'

Nanny came in, anxious, wanting to know how the fall had happened. 'What you want, M'm, isn't a drink but a cup of warm sweet tea. It's best for shock.'

'This is good for shock, too. You go along with Paul. He's the shocked one. It was lucky that he wasn't going down the stairs before me.'

'I'll bring you some tea all the same,' Nanny said obstinately.

'Oh, and tell Mrs Harper that Mr Mark will be here for dinner. You will stay, won't you?' she added to him. 'I don't want you to go just yet.'

'Of course I will,' he answered, as if pleased to be wanted.

Soon she was able to sit up and go to her usual chair. 'Sing to me,' she said. 'I find it soothing.'

So he sang an old song called 'Twickenham Ferry'. Nanny came in with the tea, which Emma made a pretence of drinking. 'I don't want to hurt her feelings. But I'd like another drink. You can drink this for me, if you want to be a hero.'

'I'd drink hemlock for you, and you know it.' He came and kissed her, and managed to swallow half the tea, grimacing as he did so.

'You're really quite a dear,' Emma said to him, 'and I only wish things could be as you want them.'

'So do I. But I won't worry you now.' He made a face. 'I think I was the one who wanted the weak, sweet tea. What a shock you gave me!'

That night, when she went to bed, the tune of the song he had sung lodged in her head and would not go away.

She twisted and turned this way and that, and fancied that the child moved.

She slept at last, uneasily, dreaming of the bus and the stairs. At four in the morning she miscarried. 'Nanny,' she called, 'Nanny!'

Nanny came in, doped with sleep. 'Fetch a doctor,' Emma said. 'Please.'

So there was never any need to tell anything to Paul.

184

'What sex was it, do you know?' she asked the doctor, who had brought a nurse with him.

'It would have been a girl,' the nurse said. Mark's daughter. 'Try to lie quietly now.'

In the morning Paul was told that his mother was ill, but that she would be well again soon. He looked desolate.

She lay back, white and bloodless, on the pillows. When Mark telephoned to know how she was, he heard the news from Nanny.

'I'll be right round,' he said. He sounded on the verge of tears.

He sat by the bed and held Emma's hand in silence. 'Don't mind too much,' she said to him.

'I can't help minding. But I'm glad you're safe. Is there anything I can do?'

'You could take Paul and Kim for a walk. Nanny is too busy with me.'

'I'll do that.' He looked relieved, as most of the beloved do when leaving a sick-room or a hospital ward.

Agnes, who had also been told the news, came round with her arms full of peonies. 'My poor darling! But it may be all for the best.' Emma smiled at this platitude, but said nothing. 'Go and talk to Mark,' she said after a while. 'I've nothing new to add.'

And Agnes, intimidated, obeyed.

Emma hardly knew what she herself had been waiting for – a deliverance? a miracle? Nevertheless, now she grieved for the daughter she would never have. She managed to cheer up when Paul came in to see her, but for the other part of the time she mourned. She would have called her Clemency, an old Puritan name, rare, but not so rare as to be ridiculous. She could see Paul bending over his sister, perhaps loving her. Or perhaps not. Only children sometimes longed to be 'only ones' for ever. She knew that she had. She had never longed for Agnes's care to be dispersed over another child. It was selfish, of course, but that was nevertheless how it was.

It was ten days before she was about again, and she still felt very weak. She let Mark come as often as he pleased, taking comfort from his chatter and his liveliness. Agnes took her for drives, once to Kew Gardens to see the lilacs in flower. Paul was puzzled. 'I shouldn't have thought such a little fall would make you so ill, Mummy.'

'Well, it did. But I'm getting over it. How's school?'

'Fine. We started Latin today and I thought it was quite fun. Scrymgeour thought so, too.' This was a bright child of the kind destined to be an academic rival in the life of another. 'Mensa, mensa, mensam—' Paul began.

Emma finished it for him. 'Mensae, mensae, mensa.'

'I didn't know you knew Latin, Mummy!'

'I know quite a lot of things. I won a prize for it once.'

'When you were at school? Did you win many prizes?'

'Only that one. Oh, and another for an English essay.'

He admired and kissed her. 'Clever Mummy.'

Nanny was away for a week with her sister. She had looked very tired. Emma was capable of taking Paul to and from school, though she often, to Paul's pleasure, succumbed to the temptation of a taxi on the way home. She also bathed him and put him to bed. 'I like it with only you here, Mummy. Though I like Nanny, too.'

Mrs Harper cooked them healthy, hearty meals, jam sponge, which Paul loved. She was a small muscular woman, rather taciturn, but with nothing of ill-humour about her. She simply liked to 'keep herself to herself', as Emma had found out. Agnes came daily to help them out with the shopping. She was blissful that Emma's problem was now solved, though she tried not to show it. Mother and daughter went to church most Sundays, and Emma did not mind calling herself a 'miserable sinner'. That, she thought, was what she was. She had trodden the primrose path and was afraid, all her suspicions rising, of the everlasting bonfire. She was envious of her mother's blameless life, uncorrupted by the flesh.

One night Mark said to her, 'Now that there's no particular point in it, I'm going to ask you again to marry me. We get on well together, don't we? Please say yes.'

So, weakened, she did say so, and immediately regretted it. But by then it was too late. He was irradiated with delight, kissing her lips, her eyes, her hair.

'I can't give you much, only love and some fun. But I'll work hard for you, believe me.'

So they were married early next year at a registry office, with only Agnes and Winter as witnesses. Mark moved into Emma's flat. 'Snug as a bug in a rug,' Winter said. 'I hope she doesn't live to regret this. But that boy knows where's his bread's buttered.' These were bitter words from him, and the only ones Agnes had ever heard him speak. She made no reply, except to say, 'Married for the third time at twenty-six. What a history!'

But Paul seemed pleased. 'I like Mark, Mummy. He sings so nicely. And he'll be company for you, won't he?'

She said yes, that was so. 'I like him better than Papa,' he said, 'though not so much as Daddy.'

'You can hardly remember Daddy.'

'Yes, I can. I remember quite a lot.'

Sylvia, who had been relieved when Emma lost the child, was now bewildered. She, who had refused him so long, had now married him for no reason. She was never going to understand her sister-in-law.

Chapter Five

DESPITE her own troubles, the events of the previous year had not left her unmoved. The continuing, desperate struggle in Spain, the abdication of Edward VIII in order to marry Wallis Simpson. She had cried a little at his broadcast, but had not been sorry to see him go. She suspected him politically. She spent two afternoons a week at the Labour Party rooms, addressing envelopes pleading for milk for Spain. She had refused, however, to join the Party, though her sympathies were with it. It seemed to her that she had already accepted too much.

Now, in 1937, she found that Mark tolerated her beliefs but would not share them. He was an intrepid fence-sitter, shaken with every wind that blew but somehow never falling off. This, to Emma, was oddly soothing, just as her husband was. They went to Rogers and Astaire films, and she found that soothing, too. When they resumed relations, she took care to take the precautions herself. She was not going to be caught another time, though she guessed that Mark would be pleased if she were. Jim Clegg was a weekly visitor. She had become reconciled with him and was ashamed of her old suspicions. He had not been in trouble again. But one afternoon, returning unexpectedly from a cancelled meeting, she found them in her bed together.

She shook with rage and disappointment. 'Both of you get out of here, and don't come back.'

'Darling, I'm so sorry. It was only the once, I swear it. And where shall I go?'

'Go to Jim's place. I'll send your things after you. Don't just sit there, Jim, get out. Mark will follow.'

They did not stir, but drew the blankets up to their chins.

'Go and get dressed. Then come and see me.'

'The Headmistress,' Jim murmured, but it was loud enough for her to hear.

'How did you know who would come in?' She could not resist this. 'Nanny? Mrs Harper? Even Paul?'

'Nanny and Paul are out. Mrs Harper is in the kitchen,' said Jim.

'You could have been caught at any time. Now, get yourselves decent.'

She waited in the drawing-room till Mark emerged. Jim had already gone.

Mark looked hang-dog. 'You didn't mean that about me going?'

'You won't share a room with me again. Nanny can make what she likes of that.'

'I'm a bit bisexual, though I like women best. I've had to live with it.'

'And I haven't to live with you.'

'But we get on so marvellously—'

'We did.'

'I swear I'll be good to you and Paul; I solemnly promise.'

As his excuses and promises flowed on, she was taken by the desire to sleep. She could hardly attend to what he was saying.

At last he said, 'I don't have to go, do I?'

She answered vaguely, 'Oh, no. I'm stuck with you and we have to make the best of things. Now I'm going to lie down, and I don't want to hear another word.'

She stretched herself out on the divan and he sedulously put a rug round her, though it was a warm day. She slept at once.

She dreamed that she was eight years old, staying with her mother in lodgings at Westcliff-on-Sea. There was an old harmonium in the sitting-room on which she had been allowed to pick out secular tunes. At the back of the house was a ragged garden, part vegetables, part flowers, mostly yellow daisies. The sky overhead was bright blue, the blue of every child's summer. She was wandering down the path. They had been to church that morning, and now she was praying. 'Please God, give me a happy life.' At the end of the path a beautiful woman appeared, a stranger to Emma. She said, 'If you're a good girl.' The vision faded, and she slept without further dreaming. When she awoke it was to find Paul and Nanny in the room.

'What time is it?'

'A quarter to five, M'm.'

'We thought you'd never wake up, Mummy,' said Paul. 'We're late. Kim was naughty and ran away and we had an awful time catching him.'

He sat beside her, gently stroking her cheek. She sat up, throwing the rug to the floor.

'You'd better go and get your tea now, darling. And, Nanny, I wouldn't say no to a cup myself.' She cuddled Paul, and thought of his dead sister. Her head was clear now and the events of the afternoon were coming back to her. Mark returned, shambling into the room.

'All right, darling?'

'I'm all right.'

She was able to think clearly. She realised that this was not the first and would not be the last time Mark had betrayed her. Yet he would be kind, good company, and would satisfy her physical needs. He was probably the best she could do.

'I'd have given anything in the world if you hadn't—' he began, but she stopped him.

'Don't dare to say another word about it.'

'I love only you. You know that. I can't help being made as I am.'

Nor can I, she thought bitterly. She remembered the woman of the dream. She had not been a good girl and she had not had a happy life. The bonfire awaited her, throwing up sparks as her father tried to trample them down. Or was her punishment now? In this world? She had never been really sure that she believed in a next one. But she and Mark would build up a life for themselves, based on tolerance and pity.

She wished she had not been born with so powerful a sense of guilt and knew that Agnes, in all innocence, had encouraged it by her own piety.

Mark slept in the spare room that night.

Next day they took Paul and Kim to Wimbledon Common, and made the long walk to Queensmere. Kim was wearing a new scarlet harness, with the lead in the middle of his back, instead of the collar round his neck. Somehow he managed to escape from them and plunged joyously into the lake. When eventually they got him out the colour of the harness had run and he had turned pink. They had to make the return journey with a pink dog, to everyone's amusement including Mark's, who seemed totally to have forgotten the events of the previous day. 'Fancy dyeing the poor beast,' said a passer-by. 'What some people will do to be different!'

They got Kim home and bathed him, but it was difficult to get the dye off. 'I liked him pink,' said Paul. 'He looked funny.' Anyone would have thought they were a happy, united family.

And they became so, or nearly. Emma's friends were envious of her good fortune, and praised her and Mark to their faces. He saw no more of Jim Clegg, so far as she knew, and his behaviour to herself was beyond reproach.

She often thought of the past, of the dancing with the carpet rolled back and Stephen winding up the gramophone, of the early carefree days on the links with Alan, of old Miss Plimsoll with her 'waste of water', and her well-meaning gifts of bolts of hideous material. Of Eric Flowers and the postcards, and then she shuddered. Paul seemed really fond of Mark, whom he called by his Christian name. He in himself was enough to keep them together. And he did so.